Holly, Mistletoe, & Midnight Snow

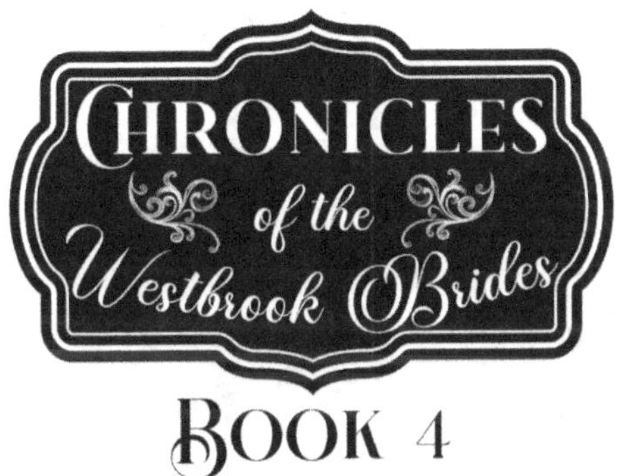

Chronicles of the Westbrook Brides

Book 4

USA Today Bestselling Author

Collette Cameron®

SWEET-TO-SPICY TIMELESS ROMANCE ®

Blue Rose Romance® LLC

"Why did you kiss me, Owen?"

*Because
I couldn't
help it...*

*Because,
Lady Althelia
Westbrook,
you have
mesmerized me...*

including photocopying, recording, or by any information storage and retrieval system, without the written permission of the publisher, except where permitted by law.

NO AI TRAINING OR DATA SCRAPING: Without in any way limiting the author's [and publisher's] exclusive rights under copyright, any use of this publication to "train" generative artificial intelligence (AI) technologies to generate text, audiobooks, and translations into any language is **expressly prohibited**. This includes scraping the internet for data from this work, any related data, or any works or data by Collette Cameron. The author reserves all rights to license uses of this work for generative AI training and development of machine learning language models as well as the rights to all derivative works.

For permission requests, write to the publisher at the address below.

Attn: Permissions Coordinator

Blue Rose Romance® LLC

PO Box 167

Scappoose, Oregon 97056 USA

collettecameron.com

eBook ISBN: 978-1-955259-63-7

Print Book ISBN: 978-1-955259-76-7

USA Today Bestselling Author
Sweet to Spicy Timeless Romance
COLLETTE
collettecameron.com
CAMERON
Blue Rose Romance LLC

PRAISE FOR...

HOLLY, MISTLETOE, AND MIDNIGHT SNOW©

See What Readers Are Saying About
Holly, Mistletoe, and Midnight Snow!

★★★★★ "I did not want to stop reading this sweet story. Such an instant connection between Althelia and Owen."

— CHRISTINE WOINICH

★★★★★ "A charming romance with a couple in love with each other but both have their insecurities. I loved their journey to a HEA"

— JANET

★★★★★ "As always Collette Cameron's novel is warmhearted and a delight."

— MARGARET WATKINS

★★★★★ "An array of stolen moments that thrum with chemistry, intimate banter, instantaneous attraction and building admiration that blooms between kindred spirits, Owen and Althelia, and sparkles with an empathetic connection that so effortlessly had me captured in the moment of their budding romance."

— SANDRA

★★★★★ "The banter between the two is great and Owen's gentleness with the horses and puppies is moving. I am looking forward to more stories with the Westbrook family."

— TERRIE

HOLLY, MISTLETOE, AND MIDNIGHT SNOW

A ROMANTIC OPPOSITES ATTRACT MYSTERY & SUSPENSE FAMILY SAGA REGENCY ROMANCE

CHRONICLES OF THE WESTBROOK BRIDES
BOOK FOUR

COLLETTE CAMERON®

GET YOUR FREE BOOK!

THE REGENCY ROSE®

JOIN MY EXCLUSIVE MAILING LIST AND GET A FREE EBOOK!

Plus Sneak Peeks, Giveaways, Contests,
Exclusive Content and More...
P.S. I promise only good stuff ~ no spammy stuff!

Scan the following QR Code to join
The Regency Rose VIP Group Mailing List
and get your FREE BOOK!

Thank you,
Collette Cameron®

THE
REGENCY
ROSE®
VIP
CLUB

ACKNOWLEDGMENTS

Holly, Mistletoe, and Midnight Snow was originally part of ***Christmas in Cumbria: A Regency Christmas Collection.***

Thank you to the wonderful authors who took part. A special thank you to Chasity Bowlin for her hard work in organizing the anthology.

For everyone who hasn't had a place to celebrate Christmas and to those who invite the lonely into your homes for the holidays. Bless you all.

ONE

Hefferwickshire House
Latham Duchy Country Estate

19 DECEMBER, 1826 ~ LATE AFTERNOON

Why did I let Leonidas Westbrook talk me into this ludicrous farce?

Taking in the ostentatious manor—every window glowing with a warm welcome—and the immaculate grounds dusted with snowfall as if God Himself thought the tableau needed a sprinkling of festivity, Owen Lockington swore inwardly.

I've lost my everlasting bloody mind.

Slinging a battered satchel over his shoulder before dragging an equally dilapidated leather valise from the hackneyed coach's interior, he caught sight of his humble, less-than-fashionable attire and his scuffed boots, badly in need of a good polish.

I'm as out of place as feather dusters at a duel.

A crooked, self-deprecating grin skewed his mouth upward on one side as he gave a contemptuous shake of his head.

Nothing new there.

How long had it been since he felt he belonged anywhere?

Since his mother had been alive.

Dour, pensive, and resembling his mother's large, rough Gaelic tribal ancestors, Owen had never fit in. It was a wonder, in truth, that he and Leonidas had become such good friends at university. A friendship that had prevailed for over a decade now, though they seldom saw each other.

When they did, however, they resumed their acquaintance as if no time had passed.

A good-sized male Dalmatian pranced over to inspect the new arrival. After thoroughly sniffing Owen's feet and calves, the chap lifted his head for a pet.

"I've passed muster, have I?" Owen scratched behind the dog's solid black ears.

The dog thumped his thick tail thrice before trotting off, sniffing several bushes, and marking his territory along the way.

Unease scraping sharp talons the length of his spine, Owen once more skimmed his gaze over the stately mansion, smoke winding lazily skyward from multiple chimneys. Yet rather than turn around on his next breath, leap into the cold, smelly conveyance, and order the burly driver to make haste back to the village as common sense admonished, Owen sprinted up the steps.

At least this year, he wouldn't spend Christmas with only a bottle of brandy and a book for company, as he'd done for nearly a decade.

Leonidas had assured Owen that his parents, the Duke and Duchess of Latham, would welcome a guest for the holiday. Wholly out of character, Owen had accepted the invitation from his only close friend after running into him in London.

He already regretted his impulsive decision, but there was dashed little he could do now. Unless he stole a horse from the stables or walked, his chance for escape rumbled down the gravel drive, leaving dual ribbons in the glistening snow.

Filling his lungs with crisp winter air, he braced his shoulders.

A week at Hefferwickshire House was survivable, even for a social outcast such as himself.

He'd trimmed his hair this morning, and the unfashionable, unruly sable locks only brushed his collar now. He'd even deemed to shave his beard, lest the servants think him a vagabond and direct him to the back of the house for a crust of bread.

Sighing, Owen rapped upon the entrance with his forefinger's knuckle and veered a glance heavenward. The gray, lackluster sky and dusky horizon portending nightfall and, perchance, more snow matched his sour mood.

The door flew open. As if Leonidas had peered out a window awaiting Owen's arrival, his oldest friend stood there grinning like a baboon.

"Lockington! You actually came." He pumped Owen's hand. "I'm delighted! Flabbergasted but sincerely delighted."

"Do you generally answer the door, Westbrook?" Owen asked drolly, stepping inside. The splendor slapped him in the face like a frigid arctic wind.

Hefferwickshire's exterior merely hinted at the interior's opulence.

Seasonal greenery with gold and scarlet ribbons adorned the elegant entry, filling the air with a pleasant pine aroma. A stunning Spode porcelain urn overflowing with cedar, holly, and fir stood majestically atop a marble-topped rosewood half table. Kissing boughs, heavy with white mistletoe berries, hung suspended from doorways by silver and gold ribbons, awaiting stolen kisses.

His heels echoed hollowly on the black and white Italian marble as he ventured forward a few more steps, unable to keep from craning his neck and gawking like a child at a circus.

Unlike many aristocrats, Leonidas wasn't a pretentious prick and had never hinted at his family's wealth. The manor fairly oozed grandeur and opulence, but his friend stood there, looking for all the world like an ordinary chap happy to see his long-time friend.

Yes, indeed. I'm as out of my element as an engorged tick on King George IV's broad arse.

"Simms, our butler, is dealing with a situation in the kitchen. A kerfuffle regarding too much sampling of brandied fruit and tipsy maids. I believe there might've been tossing of said fruit involved." Still smiling as if Leonidas had triumphed in a *coup d'état*, he shook his dark head. "I admit, I had doubts, and I swear a couple of minutes ago, you contemplated diving back in that miserable excuse of a coach."

Leonidas jutted his chin toward the rickety equipage trundling down the drive before turning and disappearing onto the main track.

So, he *had* been watching Owen.

"I did, in truth." A raspy chuckle escaped Owen. "But then I remembered you mentioned your cook made exceptional cinnamon buns, gingerbread men, Christmas pudding, and sugared almonds." He patted his flat stomach with his free hand. "I do like my sweets."

"Aye, I recall that about you, yet you never appear to

gain weight. Must be your gargantuan size." Leonidas stepped farther into the grand entry. He gave a mischievous wink. "I'd say the brandied fruit ought to be quite the thing too."

"Don't believe I've ever had the pleasure." Owen shifted his bags.

"Come in and meet the family," Leonidas urged. "You're just in time for afternoon tea, and Mrs. Tastespotting, our cook, made several special holiday biscuits and tarts. This time of year, there are always extra treats to sample."

Mama only ever made shortbread during the holidays —a tribute to her Scot's ancestry and a testimony to Beauford's parsimony. Though the earl paid their basic expenses, he hadn't been generous with his purse. They'd managed by skimping and economizing, habits that Owen had carried into adulthood and still served him well.

Speaking over his shoulder, Leonidas shut the door with a firm *snick*. "We don't eat supper until eight o'clock, which isn't typical country hours, so tea is generally quite substantial. I'm sure you're famished after the journey."

As Owen ate when he felt hungry and had never adhered to specific hours for mealtimes, he lifted a shoulder. Regardless, his stomach did gnaw rather persistently at his backbone at the moment. A sensation he'd grown accustomed to since hunger was a regular bedfellow.

Efficient, polite footmen in crisp crimson and gold

livery took his two shoddy bags, treating the baggage with the reverence and consideration worthy of His Majesty's luggage.

"Perhaps I ought to tidy up a jot first." Owen hadn't a doubt the servants' crisp livery was far costlier than his rumpled suit. However, the clothing the servants presently toted upstairs was only slightly better than the travel suit he wore.

He'd never cared about current fashion, fancy waistcoats, expensive fabric, and assuredly didn't give two farthings whether he tied his cravat in a waterfall or a ballroom knot.

"Nonsense. No need to change." Leonidas shook his dark head again, still wearing that infuriatingly pleased-with-himself smile. "We don't stand on formality around here, and you are expressly forbidden to address me or my brothers as *my lord*." He gave an exaggerated shudder. "Besides, Grandmama doesn't like her tea to grow cold."

Affection and a trace of awe leached into Leonidas's voice when he mentioned his grandmother.

Owen never knew his grandmothers.

Rubbing his nose, Leonidas chuckled. "She's quite an eccentric old bird. I probably ought to have warned you. I beg you, don't be surprised at anything she might say or ask. She's quite beyond the pale and enjoys shocking people."

"Your parents are a *duke and duchess*." Owen quirked

a sardonic eyebrow and clasped his hands behind his back. A practice he'd developed in order to do something with his oversized hands. "I find it hard to fathom that they don't strictly abide by all decorum. You are positive they won't take exception to me addressing you with such familiarity?"

"Not at all, and I think you'll be pleasantly surprised, my friend." Leonidas slapped Owen's shoulder. "My parents are genuinely warm people. You've nothing to fear or be ashamed of. No need to worry about their approval and all that trite rot that the ponces in London are so fond of."

Leonidas knew Owen's scandalous origins, that he was the by-blow of a governess and an earl.

Though, to the Earl of Beauford's credit, he'd done the honorable thing and acknowledged his bastard son by paying for Owen's upbringing and education. No more than he ought to have done after seducing an innocent girl and then dismissing her when her condition became known to the countess, who had only ever managed to produce three daughters.

How that circumstance had aggravated the old codger.

Beauford finally had his son, but Owen would never —could never—be his heir.

"I have the one thing Beauford covets above all else." Mouth bent into a poignant smile, Mama would hug Owen before ruffling his thick, unruly hair. "*You*, my precious boy." She'd kissed his cheek, the essence of lavender wafting from her pale skin. "And I love you above all else."

Nevertheless, the shame of her circumstances and the ostracism by her family had shattered her spirit, and she'd died just after his seventeenth birthday, leaving him alone in the world where bastards were as numerous as rats and mice and treated with the same abhorrence as the detested vermin.

Owen had rebuffed Beauford's overtures to visit and become acquainted with the man. He hadn't shed a tear when the old sod died four years ago, ironically or perhaps aptly, on Owen's fourth and twentieth birthday.

The inheritance he'd bequeathed Owen still sat in a bank account in London, untouched. Owen didn't even know how much the seducer of innocents had left him. He didn't give a blacksmith's damn how much it was.

He didn't want his sire's money.

Although if he didn't find the investors he sought to restart the coal mine in Workington that Owen had unexpectedly inherited from his maternal grandfather, then necessity might force him to accept the bequeathment.

Bitterness burned the back of his throat.

That thought, a very real possibility, galled him to his marrow.

He must find another way.

In truth, because of how the Lockingtons had treated

Mama, he initially hadn't wanted his grandfather's mine either. He supposed that made him the worst sort of hypocrite, accepting one inheritance while shunning the other.

"Leonidas? Grandmama sent me to fetch you. She vows her tea grows cold but won't take a sip until you return." A pretty girl strode into the foyer, her auburn hair streaked with fire and sunshine tied back with a pink ribbon across her crown. She wore a shirt a shade darker than her hair ribbon, and trousers covered her impossibly long legs tucked into men's boots.

If his life had depended on it, Owen couldn't have torn his attention away from the arresting vixen.

She slid to a stop, her blue, blue eyes round as dinner-plates and her full berry-red mouth parting.

"Lord have mercy and blow me over with a feather. You are quite the biggest man I have ever laid eyes upon."

TWO

AN HOUR LATER

Althelia pretended to listen to Grandmama prattle on for the umpteenth time about when she snubbed a Russian prince. However, the somber man perched awkwardly on the much too small Mahogany parlor chair, thoroughly enjoying Mrs. Tastespotting's biscuits, sandwiches, and dainties, kept drawing her attention.

The cheery fire snapping and crackling in the hearth dispelled the chill to the room's outer edges though long shadows outside crept inside the drapery-shrouded windows. It had been an unseasonably cold December, but the snowfall remained slight and shouldn't impede her brothers' journey to Hefferwickshire for Christmas.

Mr. Lockington munched away happily as if his tree-trunks-for-legs were hollow.

At least she thought he was happy.

So difficult to tell with his guarded expression.

He hadn't exactly smiled, but occasionally, the corners of his mouth twitched upward, and his glacial eyes glinted with a hint of warmth.

Perhaps he wasn't the giant ogre she'd first thought when he'd turned frosty green eyes upon her at her unrestrained and admittedly rude outburst in the foyer. Likely, he often received such unwelcome speculation about his size.

But really.

How could she not stare, utterly flabbergasted?

He *was* enormous.

Not just tall, several inches over six feet, but also big boned. Althelia suspected from the way his suit pulled taut with his movements, honed muscle covered his frame.

Leonidas claimed he and Owen Lockington had been friends for years, but this was the first time she had met the man. Her brother warned the family that Mr. Lockington was a rather serious, brooding fellow but kind to his core, and though large and rough around the edges, he possessed unexpected gentleness and humility in a man so big.

At least Mrs. Tastespotting would be delighted that her Christmas dainties were well received. Mr. Lockington wolfed them down as if he hadn't eaten in a week, which Althelia suspected, kept him from having to speak.

She dropped her attention to his enormous hands, then his equally gargantuan feet. In contrast to their great size, which suggested clumsiness, he moved with an animalistic grace she felt certain he wasn't aware of.

At one time, not so long ago, he would have terrified her.

Before staying with her American cousins, she'd been a timid, blotchy-faced dumpling, afraid of her own shadow. Her complexion had cleared, and she lost weight in Boston, Massachusetts. She still watched what she ate, afraid she might become overly round once more.

Of more import, those two-plus years in America had transformed her into a confident woman who had vowed never to be intimidated or taken advantage of by anyone again.

Truth to tell, Mr. Lockington did make her a bit nervous, but this was a curious sort of unease—something she hadn't experienced before and, therefore, could not identify as yet.

She glanced up, disconcerted to find Eva, her cousin visiting from America, observing her far too acutely.

Eva curved her mouth into a mysterious smile.

No one knew Althelia like Eva did, and that seemingly

innocent, entirely bothersome upward sweep of her cousin's mouth portended trouble.

Althelia speared her a chastising look that warned, *I don't know what you are up to, but stop your meddling.*

Never one to be shushed easily, Eva merely selected a piece of pound cake before cocking her head. "So, Mr. Lockington, how is it that you know Leonidas?"

Mr. Lockington raised his inscrutable gaze and set his half-eaten cherry tart back on his plate. Clearing his throat, his jaw rigid as steel, he glanced around, obviously uncomfortable having everyone's attention focused on him. "We met at university."

"Leonidas told us that." Unforgivably snoopy—one of her less appealing American traits—Eva fluttered a hand glibly and, without a hint of compunction, asked, "But *how*, exactly, did you become acquainted?"

Mr. Lockington veered a speaking glance toward Leonidas. "The first week."

Either he was as obtuse as a parsnip—which Althelia seriously doubted given the keen intelligence in his unique eyes, or Leonidas and the behemoth shared a secret.

Althelia would bet her new primrose pink gloves on it.

And that, of course, made her all the more curious to know what that secret was.

Not that she would pry. No need to when Grandmama and Eva were such nosey busybodies; bless their most convenient intrusiveness.

Pulling a comical face, Leonidas shook his head. "As Owen said, we became friends at university. That's all you need to know, cousin dearest."

He exchanged another telling glance with Mr. Lockington, who visibly relaxed at the skillful deflection.

"*I know*." Ankles crossed and one arm slung over the back of the settee he lounged in, Fletcher, one of Althelia's half-brothers, sent Leonidas a wicked grin. He was her only brother that called her Kitten rather than Ally-Cat, and she adored him for it.

She envied her seven brothers' interactions—the camaraderie they enjoyed and took for granted.

Though she and Eva were as close as sisters now, they'd not grown up together. Being the youngest of eight children and the only female made Althelia somewhat of an outsider. Not that her family didn't adore her.

They did, of course.

Every one of her brothers would protect her with his life.

Until Eva had come to stay, Althelia had been terribly lonely. But Eva had been here a year, and her parents and siblings missed her and wanted her to sail home in the spring.

"You certainly do not, Fletch." Leonidas leveled Fletcher a murderous glower, his dark blue gaze clashing with Fletcher's bottle-green eyes.

Nonchalantly examining a fingernail, Fletcher

shrugged. "Leo let it slip one night when he was in his cups."

"Indeed." Eva leaned forward, eagerness twinkling in her eyes. "Do tell, Cousin."

By this time, Grandmama had discerned something juicy was afoot. She thumped her ivory-handled cane, the many bracelets on her wrists tinkling like wind chimes. "Yes. Do. And speak up. My hearing isn't what it once was."

A flush crept up Mr. Lockington's square jaw and chiseled cheeks, and his eyes grew shuttered as he retreated within himself.

Unexpected compassion engulfed Althelia.

He presented quite the juxtaposition. Enormous and powerful, yet seemingly tongue-tied over a simple question or reluctant to divulge the truth.

Althelia suspected he wasn't just protecting himself, either.

"Mama," she blurted, abruptly changing the subject. "When did you say Lucius and Clodovea and Adolphus and his family are arriving? They missed Stir-Up Sunday already."

On Stir-up Sunday, the last Sunday before Christmas, the family made Christmas pudding. Everyone took a turn stirring the pudding and making a wish.

Althelia's two married brothers planned on spending the holiday at Hefferwickshire. The remaining brothers,

Darius, his twin Cassius, and her other adopted brother, Layton, said they would try to be here by Christmas Day but could not promise this year.

Last Christmastide was the first in years that all the Westbrook siblings were home for the holiday—thanks to Grandmama's meddling. She'd pretended to be ill—*life and death,* she wrote everyone. And her ploy had worked. The house had overflowed with Westbrooks.

At six and eighty, she remained feisty and sassy, but ill-health had plagued her this past year. Something to do with her heart, but she refused to discuss the ailment. She'd mourned the passing of her dear friend, Lady Portia Borthwick-Pickleton, last summer, which had taken a noticeable toll on the dear.

"Lucius arrives tomorrow and Adolphus the next day. I'm still hopeful Layton and the twins might spend Christmas with us too. Last year, Layton was so adamant that we all gather every year." Smiling knowingly, Mama set her hand-painted holly berry teacup on the table. "I adore it when my family is all together. Especially for Twelfth Night. There is nothing quite like Christmas in Cumbria, is there?"

"I quite agree, Your Grace. Originally from Scotland, my mother's family settled in Cumberland decades ago. One of the things they appreciated most about England was the ability to celebrate Christmas. It's still prohibited in Scotland, though many Scots secretly partake." Mr.

Lockington slid Althelia an indefinable glance, those brooding eyes probing, and her stomach whirled as if she'd been turning in circles.

Did he suspect she'd come to his rescue?

He didn't seem altogether pleased at her kindly interference.

"Then I hope you feel at home here for the holiday." Mama rose, and Papa followed suit.

"Excuse me. I have correspondence to finish before dressing for supper." She swept her regal gaze over Althelia's casual attire. "I needn't remind you that trousers are unacceptable for dining, my dear."

Now it was Althelia's turn to blush. "I know, Mama."

She hadn't changed after her morning ride.

It was wholly unfair that men enjoyed the comfort and convenience of trousers while compelling women to wear confining stays and cumbersome gowns.

"I hope you enjoy your stay at Hefferwickshire, Mr. Lockington," Papa said. "Have you need of anything, you've but to ask. Our home is yours."

Like a panther unfolding from an afternoon snooze, Mr. Lockington had risen when Mama stood.

Althelia couldn't fault his manners, even if he were as aloof and unapproachable as a Russian Czar.

"Thank you, Your Grace, but I am a man of few needs." He clasped his hands behind his back, the picture of docility, but she suspected he held himself in check.

A man of his size and strength had probably learned to do so lest he hurt someone unintentionally. He reminded her of the great, gentle draft horses in the stables—stunning, muscular creatures capable of great feats but also capable of immense destruction if angered.

Papa wrapped an arm around Mama's still slender waist—a wonder after she'd borne eight children—and guided her to the door. "We shall see you at supper."

"I need to respond to letters from Mama and Mynna too," Eva said, grabbing two ginger biscuits to take with her.

Mynna was Eva's younger sister.

As everyone filed toward the doorway from which hung a mistletoe sprig, Althelia lingered behind. She glanced at the fern-green Wedgewood ormolu mantel clock, surrounded by Christmas greenery, holly, and ribbons.

Just a quarter past five.

Yes, she had time to peek in on the puppies and still bathe and dress for dinner.

Inez, her favorite Dalmatian, had given birth to seven wriggling, mottled bundles of wonder a week ago. Althelia planned on making one of the litter her very own. It might help her loneliness when Eva left at the end of March.

There was just the matter of convincing her parents to allow the dog in the house. And, *if* she could persuade one of her brothers to let her travel with him for a year or two, the dog would provide company and protection. However, she still hadn't figured out how to convince her parents or a brother to agree to her scheme.

After straightening the richly appointed drawing room and stacking the tea service on the tray for a servant to return to the kitchen, she collected a cloak from her chamber and donned it as she exited the mansion through the back stairs.

The sun had sunk below the horizon, and twilight tinged with shades of orange and crimson hovered over the estate.

This was her favorite time of day when night settled onto the land like a lover's embrace, protective and warm. The gentle coo of the turtle doves as they sought their nests, and the occasional glimpse of a rabbit or fox scurrying to its cozy den to snuggle with its family, warmed her heart.

Althelia often sat on her window seat in the wintertime or on the terrace in the spring and summer, welcoming the shadows as they caressed the trees and buildings into slumber.

Of their own volition, her feet carried her along the well-maintained gravel track to the stables. A golden glow seeped beneath the closed doors where the horses, barn cats, and dogs slumbered.

She pulled the door open, the hinges' familiar creak and groan announcing her arrival.

For as long as she could recall, the doors needed oiling. She believed it wasn't as much the servants' failure to maintain the hinges as deliberate neglect to alert anyone inside of a new arrival. Rather like bells atop a shopkeeper's door.

Pushing her hood off, she stepped inside and inhaled the tangy aromas: horseflesh, fresh hay, liniment, and leather.

Comforting and familiar scents today, but that was not the case just a few short years ago.

How could it be that she used to fear horses but now adored them?

Because you changed, Althelia Byrony Elizabeth Westbrook.

Yes, she had and didn't regret the transformation from quivering mouse to unconventional—mayhap a trifle headstrong—woman a jot.

A dog's whining and a puppy's squeal of terror or pain drew her attention, and she sprinted to Inez's stall. A hulking form loomed over the dog and her pups. Fear clogged Althelia's throat, and she shoved her way inside the enclosure without a thought for her safety.

Suspicion and fright made her voice rough and accusing.

"What are you doing?"

THREE

A COUPLE OF TENSE SECONDS LATER

Intent on freeing the stuck puppy, and amid the poor little beggar's mewling and his distraught mama's whines and growls, Owen hadn't heard Althelia enter the stables. He first became aware of her presence when she shoved past him, almost causing him to drop the rescued pup.

Anger sparked in her blue eyes, darkened to the color of the sea at nighttime with her fright and wrath.

Accustomed to people fearing him and reacting defensively, he held his tongue. It shouldn't sting that this wood sprite directed her ire toward him without knowing the situation, but it did.

Uncurling from his crouched position, he carefully extended the hungry week-old pup, cupped in his hand and rooting around in search of a nipple. "I came in to spend time with the horses and heard this little fellow's distressed cries. He'd caught his leg, and his mum couldn't free him."

Owen pointed to a slim opening, no more than half an inch along the bottom of one wall.

"You probably want to get that fixed," he said, careful to keep his tone neutral and without a trace of accusation. "Tuck a cloth in there or nail a board temporarily."

"Poor darling." Lady Athelia scooped the puppy into her hands and nuzzled its tiny neck. "There's a dear. Mr. Lockington rescued your pup, Inez. You can stop growling at him now."

Inez wagged her speckled tail and began licking the puppy when Lady Athelia laid him by the dog's belly with its dual rows of swollen nipples. The famished little fiend latched on to a teat like a barnacle to a ship.

"I presume the handsome black-eared fellow that greeted me when I arrived earlier is the sire?" Bracing a shoulder on the wall, Owen folded his arms, which people often compared to tree branches.

"Yes. That is Apollo." A throaty, feminine chuckle filled the cubicle. "He thinks *he* is the lord of the estate.

Papa permits him the illusion. He's proud as a peacock of his pups too."

"Your father or Apollo?" Owen could scarcely credit his witty rejoinder. Humor wasn't his strong suit.

"Apollo, of course," Althelia replied with a *you-cannot-be-serious* upward sweep of bronze-tipped sooty lashes.

Owen had come to the stables, where he'd always sought refuge. He'd never been able to afford to keep a horse, but the magnificent beasts drew him like waves to the shore. He would own a horse large enough to carry his eighteen-stone weight someday.

If restarting the mining proved as profitable as he hoped it would—needed it to be. His entire future lay in that enterprise. After inheriting it from his grandfather, he'd invested every cent he'd saved the past decade and still needed investors to make the dream come true.

You could always use the earl's money.

Only as a last resort, and Owen wasn't that desperate yet.

Pray that he never was because, though humble, his self-respect meant everything to him. If he accepted the tarnished funds he viewed as nothing less than his father's attempt to ease a guilty conscience, could Owen live with his self-loathing?

Althelia angled her head, that swath of burnished hair shining in the lamplight. She stood so close he could see the flecks of gold in her blue eyes, the color of Loch Mor on the Isle of Skye.

His gut tightened, and moisture broke out upon his brow at the revelation that cudgeled him like a battering ram.

He was attracted to her.

She didn't shy away from him or avoid his gaze like most refined ladies of genteel breeding, which perplexed him. Usually, women couldn't look past his rough appearance and size, but she seemed not to notice or didn't care.

Why?

It didn't matter why.

Lady Althelia Westbrook was an enigma he wasn't bloody well going to try to unravel.

Not only wasn't Owen inclined to spend time on such a futile task, but he had other things occupying his mind. Mainly the thought that had occurred to him as he walked to the stables.

Would the Westbrooks consider investing in his mine?

Owen couldn't very well present the question as a newly arrived guest, but in a few days?

Yes. This might just be the opportunity he'd been seeking.

He'd have to put his best foot forward and call upon every social skill he possessed in the meanwhile—which, to his chagrin, weren't well rehearsed or numerous. For God's sake, his jaw already ached from the effort not to scowl and to keep his mouth turned upward, if not precisely in a smile, at least not an intimidating frown.

This holiday might prove to be quite profitable after all.

A horse nickered in a nearby stall, and another stamped its feet. Somewhere above them, a cat yowled, and another hissed.

Althelia proceeded to pick up and kiss each of the creamy pups, just now beginning to form spots on their silky pelts. A tender smile arching her dewy cupid's bow mouth, she held up the smallest before her face, a little female.

"I mean to make her my very own, though I haven't named the precious darling yet. She'll be my travel companion." She paused and glanced upward, worry creasing her smooth forehead and the corners of her expressive eyes. "You mustn't tell anyone. I haven't asked permission about the pup or traveling. Please promise me."

Oddly touched that she'd shared those confidences with him, a complete stranger, and trusted him to keep her secrets, Owen crossed an arm over his chest solemnly as if taking an oath. "I shan't breathe a word. I swear it on my honor."

"*Hmm.* I think perhaps that you mock me, Mr. Lockington." Nevertheless, Althelia busied herself, stuffing an old blanket into the crack the pup had wedged itself in. "Do you make a habit of venturing into stables?"

The unspoken question was whether Owen had permission to be here.

"Leonidas said I might." Owen stepped from the enclosure. "He knows I have a great fondness for horseflesh."

Still crouched, she tilted her head and grinned, and so help him God, Owen swore the radiance of her unfettered smile lit the stables with the incandescence of a hundred candles.

"Would you believe, Mr. Lockington, that I used to be afraid of horses? Of course, as every proper English girl is required to do, I learned to ride. However, I didn't learn to *enjoy* riding until I went to America and discovered riding astride. Now I feel deprived if I don't take to the saddle every morn."

Did she ride astride?

That explained the trousers molded to her shapely legs and behind.

'Twas a wonder the duke and duchess permitted her that breach of decorum.

Mayhap, their graces were cut from a different mold than other aristocrats, after all.

Althelia wasn't the prim, proper, hoity-toity duke's daughter Owen had expected. Something about her beckoned to him on a level he neither understood nor wanted to examine. He couldn't put his finger on what it was, but there was a genuineness, a refreshing unpretentiousness about her wrapped in a bold, appealing, pleasantly curved, feminine bundle.

Again, he reminded himself it did not matter.

She was the privileged, pampered, dowered daughter of an influential duke.

He was the by-blow of a lustful earl.

Their paths should never have crossed, and Owen was too far beneath her to entertain vain imaginations. Besides, it wasn't his nature to, and he sure as Hades wasn't about to start now.

"There, Inez. Your puppies should be safe now." Althelia stood and brushed her hands together, indecision etched upon her features. An attractive smattering of freckles across her pert nose and sculpted ivory cheeks suggested she didn't always don a bonnet.

Owen rather liked that.

She rubbed beneath her nose, leaving a smudge of dirt as she stepped from the stall and secured the door.

He checked the spontaneous grin that tried to kick his lips upward.

"You've a bit of dirt, just here." He pointed to the area on his face.

She wiped above her lip with her hand. "Is it gone?"

He nodded.

"We just acquired a new mount. A seven-year-old

gelding." Althelia veered him a sideways glance, half shy and half uncertain. "I think you would like Sampson. Would you like to meet him?"

It wasn't appropriate for Owen and Althelia to be alone. The animals hardly counted as proper chaperones. Though caution raised her head and hesitation sluiced through him, he extended an arm.

Something about this woman proved irresistible. "Lead the way."

She led him to a stall on the stable's other end, and as she walked, he studiously avoided admiring the gentle, tantalizing sway of her hips.

Most of the time.

"We've had him less than a month," she said over her shoulder. "Papa witnessed his previous owner maltreating him and bought Sampson on the spot. Paid twice what he was worth, but Papa is like that. Cannot bear for any of God's creatures to suffer."

That made the Duke of Latham a highly unusual peer of the realm. Most nobles were self-absorbed sots who didn't care a fig about people, let alone animals.

A massive black head appeared over the stall door with a glistening thick midnight mane. When the gelding's large coffee-brown eyes met Owen's, he fell in love with the big brute.

"Aye, my beauty," he crooned, stroking Sampson's glossy neck. "What a handsome fellow you are."

Sampson nuzzled Owen's shoulder in return.

"Why, he *likes* you." Awe threaded Lady Althelia's voice. "Sampson's usually more restrained when he meets new people. He wouldn't let any of us pet him for a fortnight."

Emotion clogged Owen's throat as he closed his eyes and leaned into Sampson's strong neck, inhaling the horse's scent. He made another foolhardy, spontaneous, impulsive decision, something he seemed to be doing a lot of lately.

No matter the cost or what it took, Sampson would be his when Owen left Hefferwickshire House.

When had his common sense, self-preservation, and reason flown to the wind like down upon a thistle or seafoam on the shoreline? Owen was where he was today because he insisted caution and reservedness guide his actions and decisions.

"Thank you for showing him to me." Emotion rendered his voice raspier than he'd anticipated. He cleared his throat. "He's a magnificent beast."

A tabby stable cat jumped down from the haybale she'd been sleeping on and yawned before setting to grooming herself. Horses in adjacent stalls poked their heads out to see what was happening and perhaps to demand a little attention.

"I suspected you'd like him, but I didn't expect he'd take to you so." Althelia's acute regard shifted between

Owen and Sampson. She blinked and glanced around. "I'd better return to the house, or I'll be late for dinner. My parents don't adhere to rigid rules on many things, but being on time and properly attired to dine are two."

"I'll walk with you." Owen gave Sampson one final pat, promising himself he'd pop in before seeking his bed tonight. For certain, he'd be back often to visit the grand fellow. "It's full-on dark by now, and there may be wild creatures about."

Althelia snorted as she pulled her hood over her tresses. "I've walked that pathway my entire life, and it doesn't scare me. Besides, I rather like the dark. That is, I like nighttime."

"You *like* the dark?" Owen shook his head as he fell into step beside her. "Has anyone ever told you what a unique woman you are?"

Something undefinable clouded her features in the muted light. "I'm a product of my experiences. I have chosen to let them make me stronger, and as a result, I've learned who I am and what I want."

"And what would you most like to do?" Genuine curiosity prompted him to ask.

How long had it been since Owen had conversed so easily with an attractive woman, even if she was a tempest in a teapot?

He glanced downward.

The crown of Althelia's head barely reached his shoulder, but her confidence and self-assuredness made her seem larger.

I'm not too big for her.

Owen nearly tripped over his skiff-sized feet at the intrusive and unwelcome thought.

By Zeus, he'd better wrangle his ruminations under control.

He'd only just met the girl, and he wasn't going to do anything that might jeopardize the Westbrooks' potential investing in his mining venture. Not even if she was the first female in a very long while who'd garnered more than his passing interest.

"I would like to travel as several of my brothers have done. To see the world. I've been to America, and that only whetted my appetite." Wrinkling her nose, she pointed her gaze skyward for a second. "I'm also intrigued with the notion of owning a club as my brother Fletcher does. You can imagine how receptive my parents would be to *those* ideas, so I haven't broached the subjects."

Owen *could* imagine.

Genteel ladies were expected to make a brilliant match and settle into domestic life without protest or qualms.

He rather suspected Althelia's future lay along a different course.

Nevertheless, it was none of his business.

At the house, he gave a short bow.

"It's been a pleasure, Lady Althelia."

She gave him a nascent, slightly beleaguered smile before slipping indoors.

Owen stood with his feet rooted in place for several minutes.

If he had an ounce of sense, he'd march upstairs, pack his meager belongings, and leave.

But as he'd already discovered this Christmastide, his common sense had deserted him.

FOUR

Hefferwickshire House Stables

20 DECEMBER, 1826 ~ EARLY THE NEXT MORNING

Humming and carrying several apple slices, Althelia entered the stables the next morning, coming to an abrupt halt upon spying Sampson saddled and Mr. Lockington leading the docile-as-a-kitten gelding out the opposite door.

Would wonders never cease?

"Mr. Lockington?"

Attired in her brother's cast-off trousers, boots, cap, woolen jacket, and a distinctly feminine pink and lace shirt, she hurried forward, smiling at Tobie, the young stable hand, as he prepared Stardust for her daily ride. "Please give these to her."

She handed the lad the apples and then pulled on her buff-colored leather riding gloves.

Upon hearing his name, Mr. Lockington half turned. He wore the same clothing as yesterday but had added a heavy coat and scarf, both of which appeared well used.

Was he short of funds or merely frugal? Or miserly?

There was a distinct difference between the latter two.

He didn't seem pleased to see Althelia.

No, in fact, he looked decidedly perturbed.

She turned her mouth downward.

Why the marked change in attitude since yesterday?

It would've been a gross exaggeration to call him charming or cordial in the stables last evening, but he hadn't displayed barely concealed annoyance then.

And that begged the question, *why* did he find Althelia annoying?

She'd introduced him to Sampson, the very horse he now led to the paddock to ride.

The ungrateful wretch.

Although, to be fair, he would likely have come upon the gelding at some point, as he said he enjoyed spending time with horseflesh. But he wouldn't have known Sampson's history, which seemed to have moved him.

Leonidas poked his head inside the stables, his eyes

twinkling with brotherly affection. "Ah, I thought I heard you, Ally-Cat."

She glowered at him for using her detested nickname.

"We'd about given up on you, sleepyhead," he continued, either oblivious to her displeasure or choosing to ignore her frown. "It's not like you to be late for our morning jaunt."

That was because she'd tossed and turned all night, her slumber interrupted by disturbing dreams. More frustrating, she couldn't recall the elusive nocturnal specters, only that they involved Mr. Lockington somehow.

"I'm here now. I shan't be but a moment." In a trice, using a mounting block, she climbed astride Stardust, then guided her toward the other riders.

Fletcher, Leonidas, and Papa waited as Mr. Lockington settled into the saddle with unexpected agility.

"You look well upon Sampson, Owen." Seated upon his mount, Orion, Leonidas gave an approving nod. "One of the best matches I've seen between man and equestrian."

Seemingly unaccustomed to compliments, Mr. Lockington dipped his square chin.

He might be larger than the average man, but he possessed sleek, animal-like grace and strength.

What do those rippling muscles look like beneath his clothing?

Appalled at her errant thoughts, for Althelia didn't go about undressing men mentally, she scrambled for something to distract her.

"I stopped by the kitchen." She steered Stardust to Papa's side. "Mrs. Tastespotting made cinnamon buns *and* sticky buns. They should be fresh from the oven when we return. She said there would be shortbread and gingerbread for tea today too. I do believe she loves baking Christmas treats as much as we enjoy eating them."

A light lit in Mr. Lockington's eyes, and his mouth twitched the merest bit at the mention of the sweet treats.

Hmm, was food the way to win the man over?

Honestly, for some reason, that didn't surprise Althelia.

"Mrs. Tastespotting does spoil us around the holidays." Grinning, Papa patted his flat stomach. "I shall have to watch my waistline lest I grow fat."

Still handsome and fit at almost six and sixty, there was little chance of that. He would celebrate his birthday on Christmas day.

"We all overindulge during the holidays," Fletcher put in.

Fletcher's continued presence was a distinct peculiarity.

Althelia had seen more of him this past year than the ten previous years combined. She had heard a few hushed conversations, which always came to an abrupt halt when she drew near.

Men and their secrets.

Something was afoot with his business ventures in London.

The small troupe set off at a sedate pace toward the south meadow. Yesterday's snow hadn't melted, and the horses' hooves kicked up frozen white blobs as the riders slugged along.

Normally, Althelia preferred giving Stardust her head and letting the horse race neck or nothing across the field, but today, she held the mare back. Her brothers and father weren't so inclined, and in moments, they left her and Mr. Lockington behind.

Frost clung to the shrubs and grass, causing them to sparkle as the sun's rays gingerly touched them. An intricately woven cobweb on a fence glittered with a thousand frozen jewels, and a boisterous crow called raucously, disturbing the early morning tranquility.

Cheeks and nose cold and likely red as the holly berries throughout the house, Althelia sent Mr. Lockington a sideways look from the corner of her eye but refrained from asking the obvious.

He seemed content to walk Sampson.

Men of her acquaintance, including her father and brothers, liked to lay low across their saddles.

"I can practically hear the gears turning in your mind,

Lady Althelia." Mr. Lockington twisted his mouth in what she presumed was meant to be a smile.

If so, he was sorely out of practice.

"Oh?" She arched a skeptical eyebrow.

He raised a hawkish eyebrow in challenge. "You cannot fathom why I didn't pelt after your brothers and father but are undecided whether it would be rude to say as much."

FIVE

Blast Owen Lockington for being spot on.

"I'm positive it wasn't because you didn't want to leave me behind," Althelia quipped. She sounded completely calm despite the fluttering of a dozen birds' wings in her belly. "Which, I assure you, you could not have done had you tried. I'm an excellent horsewoman."

She could outride and outshoot most of her brothers, which vexed them to no end. Laughing at Owen's nonplussed expression, she patted Stardust's neck.

"By the by, please call me Althelia or Ally, and I shall address you as Owen. We don't stand on *haut ton* formality here."

"So Leonidas informed me, but you'll forgive me if I remain unconvinced." Owen's piercing verdant glance was at once aloof and patient, as if he struggled to cast off his natural taciturn inclinations and adopt a different, more amiable reaction.

"You're trying far too hard to be affable, Owen." She gave him a cheeky grin. "I'll wager it's a terrible strain. You smile as if your stomach pains you or you need to pass wind."

His gruff bark of laughter cut through the frosty air, and she almost dropped the reins as she gaped at him.

Good Lord.

When Owen Lockington laughed, the harshness dissolved, the coarseness faded, and he transformed into a striking creature. A wholly attractive man. He'd never be considered handsome in the classical sense, but he possessed a rugged appeal she'd never encountered until now.

It caused her pulse to jump and her belly to quiver.

God help her.

Had Althelia truly suggested he needed to ... *fart?*

What was wrong with her?

"I know no other woman that would remark upon my ah—*nature*—in such candid terms." His features had softened around the edges, and genuine amusement, not offense, lingered in his eyes.

She found it impossible not to answer with a bright

smile. "I *was* wondering why you haven't picked up your pace."

"I'm giving Sampson time to become accustomed to my weight." He leaned over and stroked the gelding's wither. "I doubt he's carried anyone near eighteen-stone. I want to earn his trust, which won't happen if I overtax him initially."

"That is most thoughtful of you." His unanticipated consideration for the abused horse caused Althelia's heart to flutter and a warm sensation like hot chocolate to sluice through her veins.

Who was the real Owen Lockington?

The aloof, brooding brute or the caring, warmhearted man?

Couldn't he be both?

"What is the real story behind yours and Leonidas's friendship?" she asked without preamble.

An eyebrow quirked, he scratched his chin.

"You don't mince words, do you, Lady Althelia Westbrook?"

She lifted her shoulders. "I see no point in tiptoeing around. Directness serves me better these days."

He sighed, then leaned back in his saddle as if he'd made a decision.

"Several fellows—all legitimate sons of peers and a few with titles themselves—were teasing me about my birth and appearance. Even as a youth, I was gangly and huge, my hair unruly, and my clothing far inferior to theirs. They found me an easy target. Leonidas observed their taunting and called them out for it. They didn't take kindly to his interference and thrashed both of us soundly."

"I'm sure my family never knew that." Althelia thinned her mouth in outrage. "The cruel brutes. I hope you managed a few sound punches too."

"Aye, and so did Leonidas. Several of the buggers sported blackened eyes, as did both of us."

"Well done, you." She gave a satisfied nod.

He chuckled, a deep resonating purr in his wide chest, like a big, contented cat. "But that's not what kept the curs from attending class the next day. Your brother, the wicked devil, bribed a barmaid to taint their ales all evening with generous amounts of a tincture meant to cure constipation. The chaps spent the next four and twenty hours on chamber pots."

"*He did not!*" She giggled. "Oh, that is priceless."

"He didn't tell me until after he'd done the deed, lest he was caught, and I should get blamed too." Owen shook his head. "No one had ever come to my defense before, and we became the best chums afterward."

"Can I ask you something else, Owen?"

He eyed her suspiciously but not unkindly.

"I suspect, Althelia, you will do so even if I say no."

She rolled her eyes, then shrugged because he had the right of it.

How was a person to learn anything unless they asked?

"Probably. I wasn't always this outgoing, you know."

Some might call her behavior today forward and sassy.

"*Hmm.*" The noise he made in his throat told her nothing.

"In truth, three years ago, I was a mousey, bashful wallflower, easily intimidated and manipulated and frequently the target of humiliation and teasing. Not by my family, of course," she rushed to reassure him when his sable eyebrows arched high on his broad forehead. "But by others in the community, one family in particular."

The memory of the event that sent Althelia fleeing to Boston for over two years still caused discomfort but not the anguish and mortification it once had. She'd healed, but the scar remained—an irrefutable reminder to take extreme care of who she trusted and to guard her heart.

Across the meadows, the Hartigans' manor's chimneys stood as dark sentinels against the rising sun. Smoke slowly spiraled upward from one triple stack. Peter Hartigan was in residence—had been for a year. Rumor had it he'd been injured but that he'd recovered except for a partial memory loss.

Since none of the Westbrooks spoke to the Hartigans

any longer—their closest neighbors and, at one time, good friends—they didn't know precisely what had happened to him. Furthermore, if Althelia was any measure, they didn't care. That proverbial bridge had burned, and there was no rebuilding it had anyone been so inclined, and no one was.

The oldest son, Peter, and his sister, Leticia, had caused Althelia's torment, though she had no doubt, meanspirited and spiteful Leticia Hartigan had instigated the debacle.

Unexpected compassion shadowed Owen's striking eyes. "I'd vow the transition from a bashful caterpillar into the vibrant butterfly you are now was not without angst and discomfort."

How did he know?

Had he also endured pain and disgrace?

Adversity and disappointment turned some people bitter, cold, and toxic. In others, hardship strengthened them while enabling them to empathize with others who suffered.

Althelia pointed to the stately house, partially shrouded in mist. "That's the Hartigans' house. At a summertime ball, the daughter of the house plied me with spiked lemonade. I was so gullible and foolish back then. I believed her smiles and promises of friendship."

She peeked at Owen from beneath her lashes but detected no discernable emotion.

"I take it that is not the entire story?" he asked, reining Sampson in as a hare dashed across the track.

She shook her head.

If only it had been.

"No. Leticia convinced me that her brother Peter was enamored with me and wanted to meet me on the terrace to declare himself. I'd been infatuated with Peter for years, and Leticia must've guessed my secret." Althelia released a caustic laugh. "I have no idea what I saw in him now, but a young girl's silliness blinded my eyes and emotions."

And a yearning to be desired.

No man or boy, for that matter, had ever directed his romantic attention toward the unsure, gauche youth she'd been. In truth, other than Gregory Bancroft in Boston—who'd pursued her quite vigilantly—Althelia had been beauless.

Gregory's clammy hands, wet lips, and propensity to burp at the most inopportune times didn't lend themselves to a successful courtship. Besides, though she'd fled England for a time, she had no wish to marry an American and make Boston her home.

Even with her eyes open, Althelia could still recall that fateful night as if it were yesterday: Leticia's arm around her waist as she guided Althelia out the French windows, onto the terrace, and toward a dark corner. The stars twinkling overhead, laughter and music carrying on the gentle breeze, and a lone cow lowing.

"Peter awaited me in a shadowy nook. As I drew near, I smelled the spirits on him. He was well into his cups. In truth, I believe the wall supported him."

"'Here she is, dear brother.'" Leticia's singsong voice still grated along Althelia's spine. "'Just as you requested.'"

"Peter called me his darling love and yanked me to his chest. Pulling the pins from my hair, he buried his face in my neck.

"I gagged at the stench of spirits, and suddenly afraid, I tried to wrest away.

"All at once, Peter stiffened and shoved me away in disgust and loathing, though he still gripped my arms. 'Bloody hell. You're *not* Meridith.'"

Meridith Peterson, the woman Peter had proposed to and who refused him, breaking his heart.

"And then I knew the awful truth. Leticia had deceived me in the most vile way. Peter too, but rather than act the part of a gentleman and apologize or stay to help me, he shoved me away. Through bloodshot, drunken eyes, he squinted at me.

"'Althelia? Are you addled? How could you ever think I'd want *you*?'"

"A chorus of laughter erupted behind me, and as Peter stormed away, I stood there frozen and unable to flee, the target of every nasty, malicious denizen Leticia had arranged to watch my humiliation."

As she finished, the sun ascended past the horizon and glowed through the whispering pine trees.

Owen remained silent as a stone; his eyes steely cold.

Althelia couldn't conceive why she'd shared the sordid tale with him. Other than her family, she'd never told anyone. All this time, she'd been so careful not to trust blindly, and what did she do?

Blurt her most private secret to him.

What must he think of her?

Heat flamed across her face, but she resisted the overwhelming need to spin Stardust around and gallop back to the stables. Fear no longer dictated her actions. She'd face the consequences of her impulsiveness—good or bad.

"Forgive me for boring you with pathetic tales." Althelia shifted to kick Stardust's sides and send the mare hurtling after the others—anything to escape this horrid awkwardness her oversharing had caused.

Making a gruff sound in his throat, Owen turned those fathomless green eyes upon her. "I sincerely regret you experienced such cruelty, and if I ever have the misfortune of encountering Hartigan, I'll be sorely tempted to punch the bugger in the nose."

A small, angry tick caused the muscle in his jaw to flex, and the question she'd meant to ask him flew from her mind.

Owen Lockington—a man she barely knew—was livid on her behalf?

That knowledge bolstered Althelia's spirits much more than it ought to have done.

Eva had threatened to do much worse to Peter Hartigan when she'd heard the story. Her solution involved impossible physical contortions and emasculating the fiend.

"Someone needs to make him pay for what he did to you." Vengeance had sharpened Eva's features and tone that long-ago afternoon in Boston. "Louts like him cannot be permitted to get away with their misdeeds."

Heaven help the man that crossed Althelia's wall-flower-by-choice cousin.

"I shan't deny it was horrendous at the time," Althelia said. "But it was also the catalyst that made me determined to change. To come out of my shell and take control of my life. To never let another control me again."

Owen smiled then, a genuine curving of his hard mouth, and her heart fairly melted.

"I think you are quite the most admirable woman I have ever met, Lady Althelia Westbrook."

Then he kicked Sampson's sides and thundered past her to join the other men.

And for once, Althelia didn't feel the need to prove her prowess—to demonstrate she was just as good, strong, adept, fast, and intelligent as any man. Because the gentle giant who lumbered into Hefferwickshire House yesterday had rendered her utterly speechless and—*God help me*—had just taken a piece of her heart with him.

Now what was she to do?

57

SIX

Hefferwickshire House Stables

21 DECEMBER ~ LATE AFTERNOON

Unable to resist visiting the gelding again, Owen stood in Sampson's stall, stroking the horse's strong neck while considering the tawdry story Althelia had shared yesterday morning.

She'd faced ruination but, like the mythical phoenix, had risen majestic and glorious from the flames of her disgrace rather than permit the ignominy to consume her. He couldn't help but admire her gumption, strength, and intrepidness, even if forged by fires of difficulty and despair.

Sampson bumped his nose against Owen's chest, and his heart swelled with affection.

It seemed the horse had fallen in love with him too.

Until this magnificent beast, Owen hadn't believed in love at first sight.

Small wonder that two oversized, misunderstood creatures should develop an affinity.

How much convincing must he do to persuade the Duke of Latham to permit him to buy the animal?

Owen mentally calculated how much he dared spend of his limited available funds. His affection for the horse almost made him consider withdrawing a portion of his inheritance.

Almost.

It was too soon to broach the subject of buying the gelding just yet, but Owen suspected from the speculative glances Haygarth, Duke of Latham, and his sons veered his way during their rides yesterday and today that they'd concluded the same thing he had.

Fate or providence or God Himself had decreed Sampson should be Owen's.

The horse was an unexpected but welcome blessing— another unforeseen benefit of spending the holiday with the Duke of Latham and his family.

Lucius Westbrook and his wife, Clodovea, arrived early yesterday afternoon. The duke's second biological son seemed a pleasant enough chap, if a trifle reserved in his embarrassingly starched cravat and over-polished boots, in love with his exquisite Spanish wife.

Owen must join the family for tea shortly. Even as his mind shied away from having to carry on trite conversation, his mouth watered at the thought of more shortbread. Mrs. Tastespotting's shortbread was as scrumptious as the fresh buns he'd gorged on at breakfast both mornings.

His ruminations wandered back to Althelia again.

She'd revealed multiple confidences in the short time he'd known her. She hardly seemed the type to blather on about personal issues to random strangers, so why had she confided in him?

Each time, she'd appeared as flummoxed about her revelations as he.

Mayhap Owen had the same effect on her that she had on him, which proved highly worrisome. At present, there was no room for the distraction of a woman in his life. He had a plan and must stick to it if he wanted to achieve success. Regardless, how often did he encounter a female as enthralling, captivating, and wholly entrancing as Lady Althelia Westbrook?

Never.

And he'd never, *ever*, met a woman who looked at him the way she did.

It made him want to puff out his chest and strut about like a proud rooster.

Granted, a gargantuan rooster.

And that was another thing; his size didn't seem to matter to her, and because of that, he was less self-conscious. His stomach tightened, and his pulse zipped along dizzily, simply recalling her radiant smile and the edge of vulnerability she'd no doubt deny when she told the humiliating tale.

Owen fisted his hands so hard that the nails bit into his palms.

Had Peter Hartigan been present, he'd have planted the sod a facer and assured he never treated another woman with the disrespect, disdain, and disregard he'd directed toward Althelia. As for Leticia Hartigan, she better hope Owen never made her acquaintance.

He was quite intimidating when he declined to act the gentleman.

The stable door squealed in protest, announcing someone's entrance.

He peeked around the stall's door.

Althelia, holding what appeared to be a bowl of milk, strode toward her beloved puppies.

Inez recognized her tread or perhaps smelled her, and a happy whine echoed from the puppy pen.

"Hello, my love. Forgive me for not greeting you and the darlings this morning. I've brought you warm milk."

Noisy slurping commenced as Inez enjoyed her treat.

Althelia chatted on as if the dog was her dearest friend. "I've had trouble sleeping. Dreams of our visitor disturb my sleep most of the night. He's quite the most enigmatic man I've ever met."

She slipped inside the stall.

Althelia had dreamed of Owen?

A decidedly idiotic grin split his face.

"Sampson, my friend. Will you excuse me?" He kissed the gelding's soft nose. "I have the most curious pressing need to say hello to Althelia."

Sampson blew out a horsey breath which Owen took as an affirmative response.

Perchance, he should also consider getting a dog?

He'd been lonely for a long time. A dog might be just the thing.

Casting a scorching glance ceilingward, he scowled.

Owen James Patrick Lockington. Stop with these domesticated musings.

A horse? A dog?

Fanciful notions about a nymph of a woman?

Nevertheless, his feet took him to Inez's stall.

"Hello, Althelia."

A cleverer greeting escaped Owen.

No one would ever accuse him of waxing poetic.

Sitting cross-legged in a pretty rose and green gown, she glanced upward with an inviting smile.

Did she suspect he'd overheard her chatting with the dog?

If so, he couldn't detect any chagrin.

Although she'd always been open and welcoming with him, he still braced himself for the expected awkwardness and rejection his presence usually elicited with females.

"Come in, Owen."

SEVEN

TEN IMPOSSIBLY LONG HEARTBEATS LATER

Once more, Lady Althelia Westbrook surprised Owen with her openness and approachability.

She patted a spot beside her, which he eyed dubiously. As if sensing his doubt that he could fit in the confined space, she scooted over. "If you extend your legs, you should fit."

"Shouldn't you be getting ready for tea?" He folded onto the straw-strewn wooden planks, then gathered the little mite from yesterday, now well fed, into his hand. The puppy wriggled around until Owen tucked him beneath his chin.

He'd never owned a dog, but the idea grew on him

with such ferocity, much like he must acquire Sampson, he didn't know himself anymore.

Althelia pulled a face.

"I could say the same about you. I've already changed, but I thought I'd steal a few minutes with the puppies. Mama and Papa are occupied with Lucius and Clodovea, and I vow I heard a coach arrive just as I entered. Probably Adolphus, a day early." She stroked the puppy's tiny head with her forefinger. "He's the Marquess of Edenhaven and the future duke."

"Yes, Leonidas explained your father adopted your mother's two sons from a previous marriage before your parents went on to have six more children." He bent his strong mouth upward. "I'm an only child."

"Did you want siblings?" She cocked her head, her poignant azure gaze searching his face. "I cannot fathom my life without my brothers, though Mama might've obliged me by having another girl. My brothers are not unkind, but they call me Ally-Cat when they know I detest the nickname and often go off and do manly things together, which I'm not permitted to do."

Leaning against the planks, which squeaked in protest at the pressure of his weight, Owen crossed his ankles as he cuddled the pup. "Leonidas tells me you can outshoot all of them and are a formidable rival at archery and billiards."

"He told you that? Well, he fibbed because Lucius and

Layton can best me at pistols." She gave him a saucy grin. "*Barely.*"

Precocious minx.

Stroking the tiny puppy, he couldn't contain a droll chuckle. "Does it bruise their manly pride?"

"I don't think so." Shrugging, Althelia shook her head and flicked a strand of straw from her gown. Her frock would likely bear wrinkles from sitting on the floor and perhaps even a stain, yet she seemed completely unconcerned about her appearance. "I'm never sure whether they are proud or exasperated with me."

"Definitely proud. Of that, I have no doubt." He extended his other hand for Inez to sniff and scratched behind her ears when she wagged her tail in approval.

"I imagine my family is quite overwhelming to you, Owen, and they aren't all here yet. Last Christmas, several of Papa's brothers—he has five—and their families joined us. It was utter chaos but glorious too. Grandmama was in heaven."

Glancing upward, Owen scratched his jaw.

It wasn't a secret, but he didn't generally volunteer his tawdry origins. "I'm the bastard son of an earl and the governess he seduced. My mother never married. I have three older half-sisters, but they do not acknowledge me."

He'd run into the eldest, Lady Maristella Fernsby-Hartshorn, at Hatchard's Book Store a few years ago. Tall and thin, cold and haughty, she'd looked through him as if he'd been window glass. He still wasn't certain if she'd not known who he was or if she'd given him the cut direct.

Assuredly, Owen hadn't lain awake at night ruminating about the encounter because the truth was, he had no more pressing desire to know his sisters than they did him.

"I've decided I should name my puppy," Althelia announced.

She adeptly changed the subject as if sensing the conversation had crossed into uncomfortable territory for him. A skill he was coming to learn she seemed quite adept at. Either that, or she was sensitive to others' feelings and would spare them discomfiture.

Her consideration raised her another notch in his esteem, which had become perilously close to placing her on a pedestal.

She ran a slender finger, the oval nail neatly filed, down the pup's tiny, fragile spine.

"If I name her, it will make it harder for my parents to tell me no." Through the thick fringe of her eyelashes, she cut him a chagrined glance. "Please don't think ill of me or that I'm always so devious. Truth be told, I'm quite desperate for a companion. Eva's leaving this spring, and I fear I shall be lost without her."

"I don't think ill of you, Althelia, for wanting a pet."

The nascent smile tipping her mouth upward was a mélange of self-castigation, guilt, and rebellion.

"I've decided on Zenobia," she said with confidence. "The Greek meaning is born of Zeus, though *she* was born of Apollo."

She chuckled at her wry jest.

"I'm considering getting a dog myself." The words left Owen's mouth, and as they did, he realized he had no desire to retract them. Indicating the little male he'd rescued yesterday, and which currently slept tucked into his neck, he lifted a shoulder. "This little chap made quite an impression on me."

Althelia graced him with another beaming smile and clapped her hands once. "I think that is a brilliant idea. You can name him Zeus. Zenobia and Zeus."

"A most fitting name," Owen agreed, setting the pup beside his concerned mother.

"I'm positive my parents will agree to *your* request." She thinned her lips, doubt shadowing her eyes and turning them navy blue in the stable's muted light. "I'm not altogether certain they'll agree to mine, however."

If she were Owen's, he wouldn't be able to refuse her anything.

In mere days, this enchanting creature had begun to wiggle her way into his thoughts and heart and was fast becoming an irresistible temptation.

He ought to be horrified. Terrified. Petrified.

She wasn't part of his plan.

But she can be.

"Althelia?" Desire roughened his voice, and Inez cocked her head and lifted her spotted ears.

Althelia didn't seem to notice his guttural tone.

"*Hmm?*" she responded distractedly while peeking upward through those sweeping lashes.

Before reason could check Owen's insane impulse, he brushed her sweet, velvety lips with his.

Eyelashes fluttering, Althelia closed her eyelids and, sighing, leaned into him.

No force on heaven or earth could've prevented him from wrapping his arms around her and tasting that honeyed decadence again.

She moved her mouth beneath his, inexperienced but eager, and a ferocious wave of want made his head spin. If only she could be his, he'd protect and adore her all his days.

Impossible. Impractical. Irrational.

None of that mattered.

The sensual vixen in his arms did.

Seizing the precious moments, Owen cradled Althelia's delicate face in his hands and tenderly explored her mouth. He'd never get enough of this complex, courageous woman who smelled of spring, lavender, and wildflowers.

She was intoxicating—as addicting as opium or spirits —and he conceded it might already be too late for his heart. An organ he didn't think capable of love again after his mother died, though Sampson had dispelled that fallacy.

Mustering all of his self-control, Owen lifted his mouth but rested his forehead against hers. His blood thundered through his veins—deafening, powerful, and unrelenting—much like the flash flood he'd witnessed in Scotland a few years ago.

Her breath came in shallow little pants.

"Oh, my," she whispered, her voice sultry and breathy. "That was quite something. I had no idea kissing could be so … magical. I quite like it."

Mirth bubbled behind his breastbone, and he chuckled low. "I'm glad you liked it."

"Indeed. Very much." Her focus trailed to his lips in an unspoken invitation.

And God help him, with every fiber of his being, Owen yearned to accept. He'd halfway lowered his head to sample their deliciousness again when he froze.

The stable doors squeaked open, and the distinct sounds of someone leading horses inside finally stirred Owen to his senses. After their journey, the ducal heir's team likely needed a good brushing and feeding.

"Come on with ye, laddies." The Scot's burr held affection. "A nice brushin' then warm mash on this cold day. How does that sound to ye, my fine fellows?"

Owen angled to his feet, making certain to keep quiet, then extended his hand to Althelia.

He put one finger to his lips to indicate she also needed to take care.

She nodded and, without hesitation, slipped her fine-boned fingers into his ham-like grip.

Should they be discovered, explaining why he and Althelia were closeted in the stall, silent as church mice, might take a wee bit of doing. He had no desire to look down the barrel of a dueling pistol as the duke or one of his sons demanded satisfaction on the field of honor.

"Once Maddock has them in their stalls, he'll brush them down," she whispered, releasing his hand and picking a piece of hay off her gown. "We can sneak out then."

"Aye," Owen whispered back.

Coconspirators, they grinned at each other.

He had smiled more since arriving at Hefferwickshire House than in the past decade.

The horses' steady *clip-clop, clip-clop* passed by the stall and then turned to shuffling as they docilely stepped into their assigned stalls. The sound of brushing soon commenced, accompanied by the stable hand's murmured assurances.

Owen peeked out and, satisfied that the passage was clear and the outside door still open, signaled to Althelia that they could go, hopefully undetected.

When she unexpectedly slipped her hand into his palm, his heart toppled from his chest and plopped at her feet—hers to do with as she wished, if she only knew the power she had over him.

I'm in a bloody lot of trouble.

Hand in hand, as if it were the most natural thing in all the world, they tiptoed the stable's length. Once outside, he exhaled the lungful of air he'd held for fear of discovery and released their entwined fingers.

As they headed toward the great house, Owen laced his hands behind his back lest anyone observe them and suggest anything untoward had occurred.

It had, but that secret couldn't be made known.

"Why did you kiss me, Owen?"

Of course, Althelia being Althelia, would ask that.

Because I couldn't help it?

Because, Lady Althelia Westbrook, you have mesmerized me?

Because, although I have no right and nothing to offer a duke's daughter, I fear that I'm falling in love with you?

A grizzled gardener rounded the corner, shovel in hand, and saved Owen from answering. His weathered face crumpled into a wide smile, exposing a missing front tooth, as he tipped his hat.

"Lady Althelia. Sir." He veered a practiced glance heavenward. "I'd guess we'll have snow before long."

"Oh, I do hope so, Barret. Christmas snow is always the best," Althelia said. "But not before Cassius, Darius, and Layton arrive."

Conflict raged behind Owen's ribs.

Snow might well delay his departure after Christmas. However, the things that had been his priority a week ago had somehow faded in importance.

"Althelia?" Tall and regal, Margaret, the Duchess of Latham, stood in the entry, stunning in a maroon gown trimmed in cream lace with a ruby brooch pinned at the collar and matching ruby teardrop earrings dangling from her ears. Only a few silver threads peppered her auburn hair, much like her daughter's.

"Your Grace." Owen dipped his chin deferentially.

The probing look the duchess leveled Owen suggested she knew exactly what he'd been up to with her daughter, and guilt heated his nape.

"Come along, dear." The duchess motioned for Althelia to ascend the stone risers. "I need you in the kitchen for a few minutes before we have tea."

"Of course, Mama." Althelia trotted up the steps, pieces of straw clinging to her hem.

"The men are in the billiard's room, Mr. Lockington, if you'd care to join them before tea." The duchess inclined her head. "I'll send Simms to show you the way."

Owen detected no frost in the duchess's smile, tone, or brown eyes.

"Thank you." He angled his head. "There was something I wished to speak to His Grace about."

Make that three somethings: Sampson, a pup, and investing in Owen's coal mine.

A fourth *something* tried to shove its way to the front of that important list, but his reason had returned, and Owen staunchly refused to totter down that dangerous path.

Now was not the time, in any event.

As she led Althelia away, the duchess linked her arm through Althelia's elbow and lowered her head to speak into her daughter's ear. Probably warning her away from Owen as any good mother worth her salt was wont to do.

But Althelia, *the delightful minx*, reached her other hand behind her and waggled her fingers in a secret farewell.

Every carefully laid plan Owen had erected disintegrated at that moment, leaving him standing in imaginary rubble.

"Bollocks." He scraped his fingers through his mass of hair. "I'm in trouble up to my limp neckcloth."

EIGHT

Hefferwickshire House Drawing Room

23 DECEMBER 1826 ~ TWO EVENINGS LATER, AFTER SUPPER

Standing before the window overlooking the shadowy gardens, lustrous with newly fallen snow, Althelia nibbled her lower lip, scheming how she might formulate a plausible excuse to hurry the gentlemen's after-supper brandy and cigars along.

Perhaps she should pretend to swoon?

She toyed with a holly leaf, taking care not to prick her finger on a spine. The essence of pine and other holiday greenery filled the room, adding to the already festive atmosphere.

A mild headache had niggled behind her eyes since this afternoon, making it difficult to do anything but nibble her dinner. Still, she'd never swooned from a headache or an empty stomach.

Just as rapidly as Althelia concocted her potential emergency, she discarded it.

True, that would bring Papa and her brothers running—hopefully, Owen too—but then Mama would send her to bed for the evening with one of Mrs. Bottleknob's vile tonics, or at the very least headache powders, which would leave her groggy and woolen headed tomorrow.

In the past two days, she and Owen had managed to sneak off together several times. Five minutes here. Fifteen minutes there, and stolen kisses at every opportunity, beneath the mistletoe kissing boughs and elsewhere too.

However, it was impossible to arrange for longer assignations as more of the family arrived, and Christmas drew nearer. Up from Brighton, where he'd fulfilled his dream of opening an art studio, Cassius arrived this morning, only hours before the first snowflakes began falling.

At this juncture, it was doubtful Layton, a captain in His Majesty's Army, or Darius, a lieutenant in the Navy and finishing what he claimed was his last year in military service, would put in an appearance. Likely they'd sent their excuses, but given the post's unreliability and the distance the missives might have to travel, it could be the new year before the letters arrived.

That caused a temporary pall over the celebratory spirit, but as officers serving the King, neither Layton's nor Darius's time was their own.

There was always next year.

Althelia desperately wanted and needed time alone with Owen to explore this wonderful thing blossoming between them, which became increasingly difficult with all the activities Mama planned. For certain, someone would note their absence and remark upon it. Then believable explanations must be devised.

According to Leonidas, Owen planned to leave Hefferwickshire House before the new year. That gave Althelia scant little time to convince the dear man that they were exactly what the other needed. From the onset, he'd stirred something latent to life in her. When he first kissed her—what a wonderfully wicked thing for the darling rogue to do—everything became crystal clear to Althelia.

Every doubt faded.

Every piece fell into place, and she understood with complete clarity and excitement.

She'd done the untenable, the impossible, the most marvelously confusing, splendid thing she'd ever done in her three and twenty years.

Althelia had fallen in love at first sight.

If she weren't mistaken—*please God, I cannot be, must not be*—Owen's feelings mirrored hers. Now she must convince him to declare himself, ask Papa's permission, and then propose before he left.

Each of these was a monumental task, but not impossible.

Love made everything possible.

Time, however, proved a most inconvenient detriment to her future happiness.

Traveling and owning a club paled in comparison to becoming Owen's wife. Nevertheless, she still wanted a dog. In the evenings, she and Owen would sit by a fire reading or chatting, faithful Zenobia's and Zeus's heads in their respective laps.

Althelia had spent the better part of two days fantasizing about a future with him and sought him out at every turn. Which proved far more difficult than it ought to have done. The menfolk kept hying off to do manly things like cut the yuletide tree down while the women attended to the more domestic Christmastide duties.

Tonight, everyone would help decorate the tree erected this afternoon in the ballroom for tomorrow's annual Christmas Eve ball.

This evening, she had taken special care with her appearance. The cobalt blue velvet gown accented with gold ribbons flattered her coloring and emphasized her slight curves. Sapphires from Mama's parure set twinkled and glittered at her ears, collarbone, and wrist.

Althelia had suffered through Beatty, her lady's maid,

arranging her thick hair into an artful Grecian creation with gold ribbon threaded throughout. The tugging, twisting, and pinning had provoked her headache to a new level.

Still, nothing, not even if thunder cracked inside her head, would keep Althelia from spending every minute she could with Owen. She'd even dabbed perfume behind her ears, at her wrists, and scandalously in her décolletage before smearing the tiniest touch of rouge on her lips and cheeks.

All that to impress a man who'd been a stranger less than a week ago.

After the catastrophe with Peter Hartigan, hadn't she vowed never to let misguided affection dictate her choices?

But Owen Lockington wasn't just *any* man.

He was *the* man who'd captured her heart and who Althelia had decided she must marry.

Another glance at the Wedgewood ormolu mantel clock confirmed the minute hand had only moved three notches since she'd last looked.

She practically growled in frustration.

Whatever were the men discussing for so long?

Normally, they joined the women within thirty minutes.

A full five and forty minutes had passed since the ladies had come through for their after-supper tea in the drawing room. If she drank any more tea, she'd have to excuse herself to use the necessary, and just her luck, the men would arrive while she was away. Then Owen might be corralled into a conversation, card game, or who knows what with someone else before she returned.

Across the room, seated side-by-side on the ivory and gold brocade settee, her lovely sisters-in-law, Clodovea and Aurelie, chatted with Mama and Eva on the opposite matching settee. At the room's far end in the window seat, Aurelie's niece and nephew, Nathalie and Rémi, played with an intricately carved and painted wooden Noah's ark set—an early Christmas present from their doting new grandparents.

Aurelie's Aunt Marie had retired earlier, complaining her bones hurt from the journey and cold. Mama instructed a maid to heat her bed with a bed warmer and Mrs. Tastespotting to prepare a hot toddy for the elderly woman.

Althelia slid her attention to Grandmama, dozing in an armchair before the fire several feet away, only to find Elizabeth Westbrook, the dowager duchess, wide awake and her keen gaze behind her thick spectacles pinned upon Althelia.

Her weak-tea brown eyes alight with a secret, Grandmama Libby beckoned with a gnarly finger. That was the problem with having an eccentric grandmother with Roma heritage.

She *knew* things.

Althelia crossed the room and, after settling on the short, needlepoint-covered stool, took her grandmother's knotty, blue-veined hand in hers. "You wanted to speak with me, Grandmama?"

Leaning forward, the many necklaces around her neck clinking over her mandarin orange clad bosom, Grandmama patted Althelia's cheek. "My dear child, you couldn't be more obvious if you waltzed naked down Bond Street wearing the crown jewels."

Bother and blast.

Was Grandmama correct?

Was Althelia's preoccupation with Owen that noticeable?

It didn't matter.

She wouldn't admit her innermost thoughts, particularly when they were new, bewildering, and wondrous. "I do not know what you are talking about."

"Tish, tosh." Grandmama laughed, a raspy chuckle, like the crinkling of old, brittle paper. "I wasn't born yesterday. You cannot keep your eyes off that striking rascal, Mr. Lockington."

Althelia cast a furtive glance around, relieved to see the other women paid her no heed other than a cursory glance from Eva. Her cousin probably had her ears wagging as she strained to hear the muted conversation between Althelia and Grandmama.

"Hush, Grandmama. Someone might hear you and take your ramblings seriously. I've only known him for a few days. You're jumping to ridiculous,"—*accurate*—"conclusions."

"Bah and balderdash." Grandmama waved her hand as if a pesky insect flew about her head. "I'm old but not blind. I know what I've witnessed."

Althelia must conceal her fascination with Owen until he declared himself.

Surely, he must feel the same way.

Grandmama bent her mouth into a mysterious smile. "And I know what I've *seen*."

That caused a frisson to skitter up Althelia's spine, and she shivered, despite the roaring fire blazing in the hearth. Grandmama rarely spoke so boldly of her unique Roma gift. Such preternatural things were frowned upon by *le beau monde*, though Grandmama, more often than not, cocked a snook at Society.

It was on the tip of Althelia's tongue to ask precisely what her grandmama had foreseen when the brazen dame bent forward and whispered, "Do you suppose his willy is as large as the rest of him?"

Althelia choked on a half gasp, half guffaw.

God above.

Had her grandmother no restraint?

"Grandmama! You are outside of enough." Althelia

shook her head, instantly regretting when the motion rattled her brain around her skull. She said in a ferocious whisper, "I cannot believe you said that. You are truly outrageous."

Instead of remorse, Grandmama winked. "I do try."

"What am I to do with you?" Althelia shook her head. "Swear right now that you will not say anything to Mr. Lockington or anyone else about your fanciful musings."

"But child, I have no control over fate." Genuine bemusement creased the corners of Grandmama's eyes and sketched parallel wrinkles over her crepey cheeks.

"Grandmama. I mean it." Althelia squeezed the frail hand she still held. "*Please.*"

"I shan't say anything *yet*." Her grandmother cocked her silvery head, the usual assortment of colorful feathers swaying with her movement. "I'll wait to see how things play out."

Perfectly wonderful.

Now Althelia had to worry about her grandmother saying something inappropriate, and Grandmama *always* said unsuitable things.

"My dear, you look a bit piqued. Are you feeling quite the thing?" Grandmama pressed her hand to Althelia's brow. "You're a trifle warm, but it could be your gown."

"A slight headache. Nothing more, I—"

Just then, the door opened, and the men filed in.

Husbands found their wives straightaway, and as Althelia stood, she tried to appear casual as she sought Owen. Last in, his broad shoulders practically touched either side of the doorway, or perhaps his commanding presence made it appear that way.

Her heart skipped a beat, then kicked back into an irregular tempo. She was delighted to see he'd also sought her out with his gaze.

He shared a private smile with her.

Was he remembering their kisses too?

Papa cleared his throat, drawing everyone's attention.

"Forgive our tardiness in joining you, ladies." Always the cavalier, he kissed Mama's knuckles, and she gave him an adoring smile. Their first marriages were not happy matches, but they'd found lasting love the second time around.

"Mr. Lockington, that is Owen..." Papa grinned, as did her brothers, as they exchanged pleased, secretive glances.

What was going on?

Papa continued. "The Westbrooks have invested in Owen's mining operation, and after Twelfth Night, we shall venture to Cumberland and inspect our new project. Moreover, he's purchased Sampson, and I've agreed he might have one of Inez and Apollo's puppies."

Oh, well done, Owen.

A triple triumph.

Did that mean he intended to extend his visit until January sixth when Twelfth Night ended?

Giddiness burbled in Althelia's tummy, and she was hard-pressed not to give a gleeful whoop.

That gave her and Owen almost another fortnight together.

He traveled farther into the room, accepting congratulations from the women and shaking the men's hands. He wasn't at ease but was more relaxed than when he arrived.

The Westbrooks had that effect on people, and Althelia couldn't be happier that her family had embraced the man she hoped to marry—even if *he* didn't know it yet.

This love business was messy and confusing.

Just in case anyone noticed her unusual happiness for Owen, she sought a distraction.

"I want a puppy as a companion too. I've already named her Zenobia." At Althelia's abrupt declaration, every person in the room swung their attention to her.

"Darling, of course, you can pick one of the puppies." Papa's indulgent smile didn't quite meet his dark blue eyes. She had been unpardonably impolite and trampled upon Owen's moment. "You only had to ask."

"Thank you, Papa, but I want Zenobia to go wherever I go. Inside the house, the coach, everywhere." She held her breath as her parents exchanged an unreadable glance.

"That's something we shall discuss later." Mama accepted Papa's hand and stood. She faced Owen. "Permit me to offer my congratulations as well, Owen."

"Thank you, Your Grace."

A discussion usually meant no.

Lips pressed together, Althelia nodded and dared to raise her disillusioned gaze to Owen's.

Compassion simmered there, and instead of pleasing her, perversely, it made her angry.

As happy as she was for him, it didn't escape her that had he been a woman, none of the things he now celebrated would likely have come to pass. The tension she'd assumed was excitement only an hour ago now thrummed like a Highlander's drum behind her eyes.

In truth, she felt quite wretched.

Simms entered, bearing a tray with champagne-filled flutes.

"Ah, Simms. Your timing is impeccable." Papa gestured Owen forward. "Come everyone, gather 'round and celebrate with us."

Althelia offered a weak smile, blinking against the haziness that had descended upon the drawing room. Those little squiggly lines and dancing dots before her vision were the queerest things. "Please excuse me. I'm not feeling myself."

She pivoted to leave, but instead of moving forward, she tottered, her knees crumpling as if made of syllabub.

"Althelia!" Mama's frightened cry came from a great distance.

The last thing Althelia recalled were iron-like arms catching her and pressing her to a marble-like chest.

And it was wondrous.

NINE

Still in the Drawing Room

TWO AGONIZING MINUTES LATER

Owen hovered behind the settee he'd laid Althelia upon. When she'd swayed, and he'd realized she was about to faint, his heart had plummeted to the expensive Aubusson carpet before he bolted across the room, uncaring what the Westbrooks would think.

Her eyelashes fluttered before she opened her eyes and peered around, momentary confusion creasing the bridge of her nose.

Comprehension dawned, and she gasped. "Did I faint?"

"Indeed, you did, darling." Her mother sat beside her prone daughter on the settee and smoothed a hand across Althelia's forehead and then her cheek. "You don't feel feverish."

"You gave us quite a fright, Ally," Cassius Westbrook put in from near the fireplace.

"*Oui.*" Adolphus's French wife, the Marchioness of Edenhaven, nodded, her arms around her niece and nephew. "I quite feared for you, Althelia."

"Good thing Mr. Lockington is observant and caught her in the nick of time." The dowager duchess, appearing rather oddly pleased at the turn of events, graced Owen with a brilliant smile. "Well done, you."

"Yes. Thank you, Owen." The beatific smile of gratitude Althelia directed toward him rendered Owen mute for a heartbeat. He didn't even mind that she'd addressed him by his given name in front of her family, who all looked on with concern tinged with bewilderment.

All except for Eva and the dowager.

Those two were dual forces to reckon with.

"Dear, perhaps you should retire for the night," Her Grace suggested.

"I'll help you upstairs, Althelia," Eva volunteered but not before giving Owen a sympathetic glance.

God help him.

Was he as transparent as all that?

"I'm perfectly fine. I just haven't eaten much the last

few days." Althelia struggled to sit up. "I want to help decorate the tree tonight."

"Have a drink of water." Her father pushed a glass of water into her hand before signaling to the worried butler. "Please fetch light refreshments for Althelia from the kitchen, Simms."

"At once, Your Grace." The good fellow trotted off with such alacrity that he might've been walking barefoot on hot coals.

After obediently taking a sip and passing the glass to Cassius, Althelia swung her legs off the settee. "I have a slight headache. That is all."

"I've always found fresh air does wonders for my headaches." Everyone swung their attention to the dowager again. She blinked innocently, her eyes magnified behind her spectacles. "Owen, you should take my grand-daughter for a brief walk on the terrace."

"But, Mother, it is *snowing* outside," the duke protested, eyeing his elderly mother as if she might be slightly addled.

Not addled.

Just meddlesome; God love the interfering dear.

"I know, dear boy, but part of the terrace is covered, is it not?" The old girl wasn't backing down. "It would be a shame if Althelia couldn't participate in decorating the tree after she made so many lovely paper cutouts today."

Owen appreciated having the dowager in his corner,

arguing his case, and he recognized an ally when he saw one. Truthfully, he would need a confederate, for though he'd only known Althelia for a few short days, he meant to ask for her hand in marriage.

His soul fairly sang for joy, and happiness thrummed in his veins because of his love for her—quite an abrupt change for a pragmatic, taciturn chap.

"Yes, a short walk. Just the thing, I think." Althelia stood, not the least wobbly. "See. I'm as sturdy as a sailor upon a ship's deck riding the sea's rolling waves."

"Here, use my wrap. I'm so near the fire, I do not need it." The dowager extended a creamy knitted shawl.

Leonidas passed it to Althelia before giving Owen a considering look, the merest pleased smile teasing the edges of his mouth.

He knows.

Owen met Fletcher's and then Lucius's eyes.

They did too.

Owen didn't care who had discovered his secret. If all went well, his dearest friend in all the world would soon be his brother-in-law.

"I don't think..." the duchess began, but her husband took her hand.

"A few minutes with the doors open shan't hurt," he insisted.

"We haven't toasted Owen yet." Fletcher's droll reminder brought everyone up short.

"Can we not do so in the ballroom before decorating the tree?" Clodovea Westbrook, the exotic Spanish beauty Lucius had married last year, suggested in her lilting accent. She'd accurately assessed Owen's intentions as well.

"Brilliant, my love." Lucius kissed her temple, and a becoming flush colored her cheeks.

"It's settled then." The duke gave Owen a severe look. One that said, *I'm trusting you with my only daughter. Do not betray that trust.* "You may walk her to the ballroom's French window."

As an apparent afterthought, he added, "Simms can bring her repast to the ballroom. Cassius and Fletcher, please open all the draperies along the terrace and ensure lamps are burning high in those rooms to illuminate the veranda."

Owen swallowed as he met the Westbrook brothers' eyes in turn.

He might be huge, but they outnumbered him.

"Yes, Father." Fletcher dipped his chin before he and Cassius went to do as bid.

Althelia's family cherished her. They wouldn't forgive anyone hurting her again, if Peter Hartigan were an example.

"We'll see you in the ballroom in a few minutes." Althelia looped her hand through Owen's elbow, allowing him to steer her to the door.

Once outside, the golden glow of the room behind them and along the terrace illumined the silvery landscape, turning it into a wonderland.

Giggling, she pressed into his side. "My word. That was quite intense."

"I'll say." The tension knotting Owen's shoulders eased as he breathed in the crisp, cold air.

Softly but steadily, the snow continued to fall. It seemed Hefferwickshire would enjoy a white Christmas. There was already talk among the men of sleigh rides.

Once out of earshot, Owen stopped and searched Althelia's face. "Are you certain you are quite recovered— *my darling—?*"

He wished he had the right to utter the endearment he'd silently added. He hoped to have that right soon.

Nodding, she gathered the shawl's corners tighter. "That's only the second time in my life I've fainted."

"Let me guess. The first was after the incident with Peter Hartigan?" he asked.

Bloody rotter.

"It was, but let's not waste our time alone talking about him." Althelia turned soft, adoring eyes upward. "I'm happy you and my family are getting on well."

He put a finger beneath her chin, searching her beloved face and memorizing each precious feature.

Was it too soon?

Or was this an opportunity Owen could not let pass?

"I hope one day they might be my family too. I believe I would rather enjoy having seven brothers."

Her eyes grew impossibly round, and her pretty mouth parted.

"Owen?" Uncertainty flickered across Althelia's face, and she licked her lower lip. "Are you saying you want to… marry me?"

"Yes, my dearest love." He brushed a finger across her lips, reverent and adoring.

"I want to marry you, Althelia, above all else. I love you. I adore you. I know it's too soon, but we can wait as long as you need to, if you'll have a by-blow clod such as me. I'll never be refined or handsome or possess a sunny disposition. But I vow to cherish you every minute of every day for as long as I live, and when I shake off this mortal coil, my soul shall yearn for yours until we meet again."

Tears shimmered in her eyes.

"Oh, Owen. It's *not* too soon. I love you too. Yes, yes, I'll marry you."

They'd reached the ballroom's open doors.

Likely, every Westbrook peered out the opening, but Owen didn't care.

He gathered Althelia into his arms and sealed their troth with a kiss so scorching, it threatened to melt the nearly one foot of snow.

As Owen savored her kisses, the dowager's raspy voice,

filled with mirth and joy, carried into the crisp December night.

"We were right, Eva. It seems we've another wedding to plan."

"Hurry up, you two." Leonidas's amused voice shattered the romantic moment. "We have a tree to decorate."

TEN

Hefferwickshire Ballroom

CHRISTMAS EVE, 1826 ~ TEN MINUTES TO MIDNIGHT

Ting. Ting. Ting.

Papa tapped a knife against his crystal wine glass. "May I have your attention, please? Servants are circulating the ballroom with champagne. Please take a flute in preparation for a toast."

Slowly the guests' conversations faded as they turned their curious attention to the Duke of Latham and his duchess standing before the four-piece string quartet. Likely, those who attended the Lathams' annual

Christmas Eve ball anticipated Papa's usual Christmastide speech.

This year, they were in for a surprise.

Giddy with anticipation, Althelia pressed one hand to her stomach, the other securely wrapped in Owen's warm and comforting hand.

He squeezed her fingers as if sensing her excitement.

Her parents had agreed to their betrothal but asked Althelia and Owen to wait until spring to wed. Althelia couldn't be certain, but she suspected they made the provision in case she changed her mind.

She wouldn't.

This kind of love, though sudden and unanticipated, was a forever love.

Casting a sideways glance at Owen, she wasn't surprised to find him staring at her in wonderment. As if he couldn't believe *she* wanted to marry *him*.

"I love you," she whispered, gratified to see his intense green eyes soften with adoration.

He lifted her hand to his mouth, murmuring, "And I love you, my heart," before grazing her knuckles with his lips. "I don't have an engagement ring for you yet, darling."

"I do not care." And Althelia didn't.

A ring merely symbolized to others what she treasured in her heart.

"Have I told you how beautiful you are tonight?"

Owen's gaze held male appreciation and a promise of something much more intimate. "Pink becomes you."

"Yes, you have, and pink is my favorite color." She hugged his arm to her chest. "You look quite dashing too."

She had no idea how they'd managed it, but Owen wore a new ebony suit, complete with a holly-berry red waistcoat. Undoubtedly, a tailor's purse was much heavier for completing the difficult task in record time.

"Everyone. My duchess and I have a wonderful announcement." Papa glanced around until he spied Althelia and Owen and motioned them forward. "Come, come, children."

Astonishment followed by delight skittered across Owen's rugged features.

Althelia could've hugged her father for his consideration and would later on.

Her parents would treat Owen, a bastard orphan, as their own. He would finally have the love, acceptance, and family his birth had denied him.

Althelia's heartbeat accelerated as Owen led her to the front of the room, and her family formed a semi-circle behind them.

Once before, at a similar ball, she had faced a crowd, humiliated and defeated. This time, with this remarkable man at her side, nothing and no one could make her feel anything but ecstatic.

"Family and friends." Beaming, Father lifted his glass.

"Permit me to announce the betrothal of my daughter, Lady Althelia, to Owen Lockington."

Oohs and aahs followed by polite applause swelled around the glittering ballroom, lit by hundreds of beeswax candles suspended from crystal chandeliers.

Leonidas slapped Owen's shoulder. "I expect to be asked to be the best man."

"I wouldn't dream of having anyone else," Owen assured him.

Althelia hugged Eva, trying unsuccessfully not to cry. "And, Eva, I wish you to be my maid of honor."

"Nothing would make me happier." Eva blinked back tears. "Except castrating Peter Hartigan," she whispered fiercely in Althelia's ear.

"Don't continue to be offended on my account, Eva." She searched her cousin's earnest gaze. "I'm happy. Peter is part of my past."

Eva gave a tight nod.

"Sir, might I steal my future bride for a breath of fresh air?" Owen asked Papa.

"More likely, my future grandson wants to steal a few kisses." Grandmama's comment earned a round of amused chuckles.

She was correct, but she needn't announce Owen's intentions.

"Grandmama, you are incorrigible." Althelia kissed her grandmother's papery cheek. "But I adore you for it."

"Get on with you." Grandmama swung her cane toward the French windows, open to allow the night air to cool the sweltering ballroom, and above which hung a kissing bough of holly and mistletoe.

At the threshold, as the clock chimed the midnight hour, Owen drew Althelia to a stop beneath the bough. He pointed outside. "It's snowing again. Are you certain you won't get chilled?"

Happier than she'd ever been, Althelia cast off convention and gave the kissing bough a speculative look.

"Holly, mistletoe, and midnight snow. What could be more perfect?" Then in front of her amused family and the slightly shocked guests, just as the orchestra struck the first chords of the annual midnight Christmas waltz, she raised onto her tiptoes and kissed her betrothed.

EPILOGUE

Belforton Hall
Harrington, Cumberland, England

EARLY APRIL 1828 ~ LATE EVENING

T*his is contentment.*

Sitting on the floor, her back resting against Owen's wide chest and idly rubbing Zenobia behind the ears, Althelia drowsily watched the waning fire. Too comfortable to move, she sighed as he traced little circles behind her left ear and down her neck.

Zeus sprawled across the hearth, his head resting on Owen's ankle.

That Christmas season she'd first met and fallen in love with her husband, Althelia had envisioned a similar moment. Married just over a year and happy beyond measure, she now lived that dream.

Nine months ago, she'd finally persuaded Owen to accept his inheritance from his father. For the suffering he'd endured, he deserved much more than the fifty thousand pounds his sire had left him, which had swelled considerably with interest.

Owen had conceded to use the funds to purchase Belforton Hall to provide them a home and a future. They used Althelia's substantial dowery for the refurbishing of the house and stables where Stardust and Sampson, who had become inseparable, had adjacent stalls.

The investments from Papa, her brothers, and a portion of her dowry helped get the Lockington Coal Mine running again. Owen's keen but fair management had also seen a profit the first year.

"I received a letter from Eva today," Althelia murmured sleepily, curving her mouth into a half smile when Owen pressed a warm kiss to her crown.

Lord, how she loved this gentle giant of a man.

"Oh?" He sounded just as drowsy as she did. "I still cannot believe she married that rotter."

Owen hadn't entirely forgiven Peter Hartigan, though he managed to be grudgingly polite at Eva and Peter's wedding last year. Only because Leticia Hartigan hadn't received an invitation.

The Scottish Mahogany long-case clock struck half an hour past midnight.

Althelia really ought to go to bed.

"She says more snippets of Peter's memory have returned." Sighing again, she unfolded her legs, causing Zenobia to peek at her with chocolatey eyes and thump her dappled tail.

"*Hmph.*" Owen gave a noncommittal grunt.

Althelia shifted until she kneeled before him and cupped his dear face. "You don't have to like him, but I shall visit my cousin, so you'll have to come to terms with Peter. If I can forgive him, then you can too."

"I cannot refuse you anything, my darling wife."

A grudging smile tugged Owen's mouth upward, and his smoldering glance warned his fatigue had transformed into something else altogether.

No longer sleepy either, Althelia rose and extended her hand. "Let's go to bed, shall we?"

Owen's knowing look heated her blood.

"The dogs stay here tonight." His twitching mouth belied the scowl he directed at the Dalmatians. "I have no wish to awaken to slobbery kisses again."

"Only my kisses, my darling?"

"Ever only your kisses," Owen purred before scooping her into his arms.

I hope you enjoyed a romantic holiday historical escape to times gone by for a few hours with Owen and

Althelia. If you liked their story, please consider leaving a review.

I hope you enjoyed
HOLLY, MISTLETOE, AND MIDNIGHT SNOW
and following the romantic journey
of Owen and Althelia.
If you'd like to leave a review please
scan the following QR Code.

Keep reading for a FREE PREVIEW of
THE WALLFLOWER'S MIDNIGHT WALTZ,
Book 5
Chronicles of the Westbrook Brides Series...

SCAN HERE TO LEAVE A REVIEW FOR
"HOLLY, MISTLETOE, AND MIDNIGHT SNOW"

FROM THE DESK OF
COLLETTE CAMERON®

One historical fact I must address is Cumbria itself. The county of Cumbria didn't exist until 1974 when a local government act brought the counties of Cumberland and Westmoreland together. However, ancient Cumbria (established around 550 AD) is a different matter. Once a powerful Celtic kingdom of the British Isles, ancient Cumbria, also known as Rheged, was located in the northwest corner of England, in what is roughly present-day Cumbria. A Regency anthology set in actual Cumbria wasn't possible, but fortunately, with imagination, anything *is* possible.

I hope you'll forgive this small historical inaccuracy.

My research also led me to explore the Gaels—ancient ancestors of the Scottish Highlanders. The Gaels were Celtic people who settled in parts of central Europe,

Anatolia, Italy, France, Belgium, and Hispania. From there, they branched into the Byronic and Gaelic linguistic categories and are known to have inhabited ancient Gaelic regions in Ireland. Around the fifth century, the Gaelic people from Ireland immigrated to parts of Scotland.

In 1560, Scotland's kirk (church) prohibited the extravagant and often pagan practices of Christmas, though it wasn't until 1583 that yuletide officially ceased. Many Scots secretly defied the church and continued celebrating Christmas, but not without persecution. In 1712, the ban was officially lifted, but that didn't mean the church didn't continue to frown upon yuletide revelry. Still afraid of recriminations, Scots quietly celebrated the holiday until 1958, when December 25 became a national holiday.

Hugs,
Collette Cameron®

USA TODAY BESTSELLING AUTHOR
COLLETTE CAMERON
The Wallflower's Midnight Waltz
Revenge of the Wallflowers

Landford Park Ballroom

31 DECEMBER, 1826 ~ QUARTER OF TWELVE

Resting an ebony-clad shoulder against the ballroom's door frame, Peter surveyed his hundred or so masked guests. Resplendent in their evening finery, draped in jewels, and swathed in the finest silks, satins, and wools available, they paraded about the ballroom.

While many attendees had come in costume, others such as himself and Leticia, had chosen to only wear a mask or domino. The mélange was a grand spectacle, indeed.

Hundreds of beeswax candles illuminated the sanded

dance floor and the ten-foot gilded mirrors on the ballroom's far side. He'd spared no expense for tonight—his re-entry into Polite Society—after nearly losing his life. Or so he explained to the guests as they greeted him earlier when they inquired about what had prompted his New Year's Eve masquerade ball.

Searching the ballroom again, he swallowed down another wave of disappointment.

The Westbrooks were not among the attendees.

Not the Duke and Duchess of Latham. Not Althelia Westbrook or her betrothed, nor any of the Westbrook brothers. He knew for a fact that several had been at Hefferwickshire House for Christmastide too.

A servant at the ducal manor was a sister to one of his maids, and he'd stooped so low as to encourage Milly to pry information from the other servant. He even rewarded her spying with an extra coin for her efforts.

That was how Peter had learned of Althelia's betrothal.

That she had found love brought him profound relief —not absolution, but knowing she was happy reduced his guilt a smidgeon.

Though Peter hosted the ball, an odd detachment, almost a sense of exclusion, cocooned him. As if he were an outsider and no longer a member of the elite society his parents had fought so hard to become a part of.

Sweeping his gaze over the crowd once more, he released a long, controlled breath.

Until this afternoon, he maintained a foolish hope that the Westbrooks would respond to his invitation. More than once, he'd considered riding over to Hefferwickshire House and inquiring in person if the Westbrooks planned to attend.

It wasn't done, of course.

Decorum demanded he await their reply.

That no one had even bothered to decline his invitation said a great deal.

Should he encounter them in public, they would no doubt give him the cut direct.

Was he stupid to try to rectify the wrong he had committed?

More on point, were his motives pure and not self-serving?

Was his desire for atonement genuine or merely absolution for his guilt? A guilt so weighty and cumbersome that he doubted Hercules could have stood under the monumental burden.

Yes, he admitted, clenching his jaw and curling his fists into tight balls. Selfishness motivated him in part. He *must* make amends so he could forgive himself and move on with his life as Althelia had done.

But it was more than that.

Rebuilding his reputation, regaining the trust of

friends and family, and earning redemption proved powerful catalysts as well.

He did not expect the relationship with the Westbrooks to be restored, but he had hoped for civility and a degree of healing.

For yourself or Althelia?

Why couldn't it be both?

Fear's talons clawed relentlessly at his stomach, and his palms grew moist in his white gloves.

I might not gain the redemption I crave.

Then what?

Would he turn back to the bottle?

Use spirits to dull his senses once more?

He gave a vicious shake of his head.

No. No. *NO.*

God forbid.

Absently running his finger over his scar, his attention alighted on a vaguely familiar woman attired completely in white, from the elaborate wig atop her head, threaded with strings of pearls and topped with several white ostrich feathers, to the slippers peeking from beneath the rows of lace along her gown's hem.

Many other guests had come in costume as well, though he couldn't discern exactly what her attire signified...until she turned slightly, revealing a pair of dainty, gossamer wings attached to her back.

An angel.

How appropriate.

Their gazes met across the room, and a nascent smile bloomed on her pink rosebud mouth.

A scintillating current jolted Peter to his toes. Long dormant masculine interest stirred deep in his belly. No woman had caught his attention since Meridith.

Who was this mystery woman?

Who had she come with?

Leticia sidled up to him, the usual smug half-smile curving her thin lips, doing nothing to enhance her plainness.

What had made his sister into such a vile human being?

He had not invited her to the ball, but somehow, she had learned of the event and had appeared two days ago with their arthritic, nearsighted, and with a propensity for flatulence that rivaled dairy cattle, Aunt Hattie Effingham in tow. He'd almost yielded to the burning temptation to send the troublesome baggage that was his sister, packing.

Still, this was Leticia's childhood home too, and he did not remember what part, if any, she had played in Althelia's humiliation.

"I am surprised but willing to admit your little soirée appears to be a success, brother." Leticia skimmed her critical focus over the milling crowd, an undercurrent of disdain shadowing her sharp features. "I cannot help but wonder if most of the guests came out of morbid curiosity. You have been such an enigma this past year."

Peter skewed an eyebrow upward.

Leticia always managed a backhanded insult beneath the veneer of a compliment.

A practiced pout turning her mouth downward, she slapped his arm with her maroon and silver lace fan. "I do not see the Duke and Duchess of Latham and their enormous brood. Do you suppose Althelia is still a blotchy-faced, frizzy-haired dumpling?"

Venom seeped into the last sentence.

Why did Leticia bear such ill will toward Althelia Westbrook?

He opened his mouth to tell her that from all accounts, Althelia had blossomed into a beauty—a fact Leticia would choke on as nature had not been as benevolent to her—but before he could speak, someone else did.

"No. She is not."

In unison, they turned to face the fascinating woman in all white.

Her pretty mouth curved upward pleasantly enough, but behind her white lace mask, blue sparks lit her eyes. Attention focused on Leticia, she deliberately opened and shut her fan, using the language of the accessory to convey her thoughts.

You are cruel.

Peter barely kept his grin of approval in check.

"Althelia has become a beautiful and confident young woman," the mystery woman said. "She is recently betrothed."

Leticia narrowed her eyes, her features gone hard. "I do not believe I have had the *pleasure...*"

So, she did not have a clue who the angel was, either.

The mystery woman slid him a sideways glance, a mixture of humor and challenge in the depths of her azure eyes.

"Ah, you would have me reveal my identity? *Tsk, Tsk.* Poor form." She flicked the fan back and forth as if chastising an errant child and shook her head, causing the feathers topping her wig to sway. "Surely you know better. It is not midnight yet. I shall keep my secret a while longer, I think."

"I do not believe we are unmasking until two," Peter offered, not the least disturbed by the eviscerating glower his sister speared him. Never mind that until five seconds ago, the unmasking *would* have occurred at midnight.

"So I can remain anonymous a while longer. Excellent." An enigmatic smile curved the angel's mouth upward. Nevertheless, the hardness in her brilliant blue eyes did not abate as she took Leticia's measure from head to toe.

Fascinating.

Leticia pursed her mouth tighter than a beggar's purse

strings before giving a toss of her head and stalking away without another word.

His sister always indulged her ill temper, not caring how unflattering it was or who she hurt with her cutting remarks. Their parents had constantly ignored her nastiness and pandered to her demands rather than address her unpleasant temperament. As a result, she'd become bolder and more malicious in her behavior over the years.

A bubble of laughter formed in his chest, and a chuckle escaped him.

It was about time his sister had her comeuppance.

It wasn't often that Leticia did not have the last word.

"Please disregard my sister's prying." Still grinning, he examined the pretty young woman. "She is unaccustomed to not getting her way."

The angelic figure lifted a delicate shoulder. "'Tis of no consequence."

The string quartet's lilting strings announced the midnight waltz.

"May I have this dance?" Peter extended his hand. "Unless your dance card is full."

That actual possibility sent his good humor plummeting to the floor.

A winsome smile bent her mouth again.

The faint essence of lilacs and jasmine wafted upward, teasing his nostrils.

Who was this delightful treasure?

"I have only just arrived," came her husky reply. "My dance card is empty."

And just like that, Peter's spirits soared once more, but not before he mentally filed away the mention of her late arrival. Hastings, his butler, would likely know who she arrived with, for surely a young woman this lovely had not come alone.

'Twould be scandalous to do so.

"Then I would be honored to be the first to partner you." For the first time in a long while, guilt did not beleaguer Peter. Something far lovelier and tantalizing held his attention.

*I hope you enjoyed this **FREE PREVIEW** of*
THE WALLFLOWER'S MIDNIGHT WALTZ
Book 5
Chronicles of the Westbrook Brides Series.
If you'd like to keep reading
please scan the following QR Code.

SCAN HERE TO GET "THE WALLFLOWER'S MIDNIGHT WALTZ"

GIGGLES ARE GUARANTEED

COLLETTE'S CHERIS READER GROUP

If you love to chat about all things romance-book related and enjoy taking part in fun and engaging live events, contests, and giveaways join **Collette's Chèris VIP Reader Group,** my exclusive private book group on Facebook.

Giggles are guaranteed!

Hope to see you there,

Collette Cameron®

Please scan the following QR Code to join:

YOU ARE CORDIALLY INVITED TO JOIN
COLLETTE'S
THERIS
VIP
READER
GROUP

DUKES COME CALLING
A Sensual Marriage of Convenience
Regency Historical Romance

FOR THE LOVE OF AN EARL (Wicked Earls' Club)

A Humorous Aristocrat and Wallflower

Regency Romance Adventure

Earl of Wainthorpe — Book 1

Earl of Scarborough — Book 2

Earl of Keyworth — Book 3

Earl of Renshaw — Book 4

HEART OF A SCOT

A Passionate Enemies to Lovers

Scottish Highlander Historical Mystery

Romance Adventure

To Love a Highland Laird — Book 1

To Redeem a Highland Rogue — Book 2

To Seduce a Highland Scoundrel — Book 3

To Woo a Highland Warrior — Book 4

To Enchant a Highland Earl — Book 5

To Defy a Highland Duke — Book 6

To Marry a Highland Marauder — Book 7

To Bargain with a Highland Buccaneer — Book 8

A Christmas Kiss for the Highlander — Book 9

HIGHLAND HEATHER ROMANCING A SCOT:

CASTLE BRIDES

A Passionate Enemies to Lovers Second Chance

Scottish Highlander Mystery Romance

Heart of a Highlander — Prequel

The Viscount's Vow — Book 1

The Highlander's Heiress — Book 2

The Earl's Enticement — Book 3

Triumph and Treasure — Book 4

Virtue and Valor — Book 5

Heartbreak and Honor — Book 6

Scandal's Splendor — Book 7

Passion and Plunder — Book 8

Wishes and Wonder — Book 9

A Yuletide Highlander — Book 10

SECRETS OF SCANDALOUS LADIES

A Romantic Class Difference Forced Proximity

Regency Romance with Aristocrats

A Lady, A Kiss, A Christmas Wish — Book 1

No Lady for the Lord — Book 2

Love Lessons for a Lady — Book 3

His One and Only Lady — Book 4

Never a Proper Lady — Book 5

Lady Tempts a Rogue — Book 6

THE CULPEPPER MISSES

A Humorous Wallflower Family Saga

Regency Romantic Comedy

The Earl and the Spinster — Book 1

The Marquis and the Vixen — Book 2

The Lord and the Wallflower — Book 3

The Buccaneer and the Bluestocking — Book 4

The Lieutenant and the Lady — Book 5

THE HONORABLE ROGUES®
A Second Chance Redeemable Rogue
and Wallflower Regency Romance

A Kiss for a Rogue — Book 1

A Bride for a Rogue — Book 2

A Rogue's Scandalous Wish — Book 3

To Capture a Rogue's Heart — Book 4

The Rogue and the Wallflower — Book 5

A Rose for a Rogue — Book 6

'Twas the Rogue Before Christmas — Book 7

A Rogue Worth the Risk — Book 8

About the Author

USA Today Bestselling author Collette Cameron® is renowned for her captivating, humorous, and heart-warming Scottish and Regency historical romance novels. With over 65 published titles, over 1.4 million books sold around the world, and multiple writing awards to her credit, Collette is a well-known author in the world of historical romance. Readers love her witty and relatable characters including daring rogues, dashing scoundrels, and the strong and spirited heroines who capture their hearts. From the rugged highlands to the refined drawing rooms of Regency England, Collette's novels will transport you to another time and place, where love and adventure are just a page away.

Collette's Sweet-to-Spicy Timeless Romances® are the perfect escape for readers looking for romantic escape, poignant inspiration, engaging humor, and entertaining stories.

Based in the Pacific Northwest, Collette is surrounded by the lush greenery and rainy skies that inspire her writing. She dreams of one day splitting her time between the Pacific Northwest and Scotland. In the meantime, she indulges in her love of all things cobalt blue, dachshunds, chocolate, and of course, crafting her next historical romance.

Blue Rose Romance® LLC
PO Box 167
Scappoose, Oregon 97056 USA
collettecameron.com

If you haven't joined Collette's exclusive mailing list scan the folloing QR Code to sign up!
You'll get access to exclusive content, sneak peeks, contests, giveaways, and more...
(P.S. No spammy stuff.)

Follow Collette on social media.
Scan the following QR Code:

www.ingramcontent.com/pod-product-compliance
Lightning Source LLC
Chambersburg PA
CBHW071939190726
48293CB00004B/1287